GABRIEL, THE
TRAINING OF AN ANGEL

A Novella

Diane Rosier Miles

Contact the author at dianerosiermiles@gmail.com.
ISBN 1547068183
ISBN 13: 9781547068180

DEDICATION

This book is dedicated to my husband, Ed, who loved me, believed in me, and provided for me while I wrote it. God made Ed the earthly source of everything good that has happened to me for over thirty years. I am so grateful for my husband and his willingness to entwine his life with my own. I also want to recognize my son, Eddie, who is a fellow night owl. His spiritual insights are uncommon for a young man his age, and they have been the inspiration for many of my story ideas. Thanks to Eddie for his love and midnight cheeseburger runs.

ACKNOWLEDGMENTS

I am thankful for the encouragement of my local church family, especially the women of our book club. I would also like to express appreciation to my beta readers for their warm friendship and excellent editorial suggestions. I am likewise deeply grateful to my Facebook friends for their witty camaraderie and good will.

To all, your enthusiasm for my writing means more to me than you know.

PROLOGUE

The Scriptures say there will be no end to the making of books, which encourages me to tell my story. I do not compete with the intrepid Saint Paul, who wrote such gripping tales that the Gentiles followed him by the thousands. Nor do I rival Moses, who held the Israelites spellbound with stories of privately meeting with God. I do not challenge Martin Luther, who hammered his views to doors and then composed his emotions (and hymns) to the tunes of alehouse songs.

I am only a heavenly messenger with memories. My book wants merely a cubbyhole in heaven's library. I'm content to tell my tale in the knowledge that I fulfilled the herald's task to which I was called by God as a newly created angel. If my writing is ever bound into a book, perhaps it will aid others in their own work for the Lord, including any beings besides angels and saints Most High has yet to create. Or perhaps when the New Jerusalem is brought down to the awaiting Earth, even the animals there will be so renewed as to be able to read and learn from my humble scratching. You never know. God never runs out of ideas.

In order that I might summon up the best of my creativity, I have decided to make writing this memoir an alfresco effort. The roses' sweet fragrance enlarges my vocabulary—a circumstance that I don't understand but do appreciate. As I recount my story here in paradise, now as an angel of great age, I will do my best to tell the truth and the lessons of my mission. I am not afraid to appear in an unflattering light for a while, or to admit that I needed to grow in knowledge and faith. I was young once, falling over my own wings in naïveté.

It was my privilege to undertake for the Lord the announcement of his imminent coming to Earth for mankind's sake. God's arrival inflamed many, some to lifetimes devoted to mercy and magnanimity, and others to acts of barbarism. Few were neutral. Regrettably, many of God's supposed followers pursued both the light and the dark in the same lifetime, contemptuous of the voice of the Spirit within them.

Even the gathering of the Word into the canon brought mortals to dissension and bloodshed. I did not write a syllable of that great work. I was not asked to contribute or compile. I was instructed to announce—and to postpone fulfilling my own authorial aspirations until now. Hence, my expertise is in delivering messages. I was to carry them swiftly, and I made observations along the way.

One does not undertake momentous errands without preparation, lest the assignment fail due to under-qualification in the servant. It's my belief that this memoir reflects God's wisdom in training me for a responsibility that had no equal among the angels. I'm not sure I would have been of much use to the Lord if I had not been introduced, in small doses, to what was at stake in his coming to Earth for man. In the beginning of my task, surely I had no clue. I did not suspect that humanity's condition was hopeless without God's intervention.

Let me make myself comfortable here on the mossy banks of the Lake of Insight, and I'll begin my story. As I write, the snow geese are practicing their homing skills over the glistening water, so that when they emerge on Earth, fresh and downy from their eggs, they will be able immediately to travel without assistance over enormous stretches of sunlit skies and moonlit clouds in precise, seasonal journeys that intimidate even the most expert of human navigators. The mystery is, of course, that the geese were trained for their travels before ever leaving heaven's air, having the Lord's map of his Earth imprinted into their silken feathers while they practiced and mastered their steering skills with Insight.

So it was with my journey and me. It was almost the same right down to the feathers, although mine were not damp with Lake Insight's dew when I came to awareness. I, too, was trained. I, too, knew what it was to need guidance when far from home. Our Father required of me a year among the mortals, a kind of apprenticeship for credentials, which God had planned before Christ's coming to help me deduce the weight of the greetings I would carry to human souls. The Lord did not want me to romanticize humanity's fallen state, or to mistake his coming to Earth for man's salvation as a trip without grievous costs for him, which I might have done if I'd only visited Earth for an hour or two, in good weather, perhaps when people had had a rare calm day and plenty to eat. No, my prolonged involvement in messy humanity was required, so that I might experience the true state of the mortals' crisis. God had a plan.

When I first opened my eyes to serve the Lord, I came to consciousness kneeling at the solid sapphire throne of the Ancient of Days. God was on fire, having hair of white wool and eyes ablaze. I can say no more about God's appearance because, though I now know it well, it is not permitted of me to break heaven's secrets, for the Day of Judgment has not yet come. Moreover, God's physical manifestation is not the most important question with which readers should occupy themselves, and indeed his state is a spiritual, not a physical, orientation that is far above understanding.

As I awoke initially before Father God, consciousness confused me. My breath filled my chest in short apprehensive gasps, as a bird might quiver with trepidation in the hand about to set it on a perch. The white light cast by the Father engulfed me totally, producing a permanent halo above my head as a shining shadow, but soon my confusion subsided into absolute trust, and my eyes, at first overwhelmed, became accustomed to the Shekinah brilliance. I was awestruck, not knowing my purpose for living but full of an ardent desire to please the one I instantly knew as my creator.

Immediately as I came to life, there was the new feeling of words reverberating in me, the words of God. Instinctively, I knew relationship with him would come through words. I did not know, then, that a messenger angel such as myself would need to be intimately familiar with the power of words. It is not an overstatement to say that words, used in the service of God, were the reason for my living. During my first moments of existence, my cells still resonated with the Father's words, as a singing bowl will continue to sound after striking.

Self-awareness gradually awakened me fully. I could reason. I could question. I discovered that I held an inscribed chalice of wine and a mound of soft bread, whose symbolism I did not understand at the time. Oh, I was young! I remember hearing the thunder in this, the throne room of God. I recoiled at the flashes of notched lightning, which illuminated the smoking incense leaping with sparks from burnished bowls. Looking up, I saw that I knelt in a roofless space studded with points of light I now know as the Third Heaven. This space echoed with exuberant praises to Yahweh. I searched for the source of the shouting.

Four frightful creatures cried out in a startling quartet. Each creature was bedecked with eyes that were like my own but innumerable, and these eyes looked with intense focus in all directions to ensure that nothing evil should approach Most High. The creatures also had wings like mine, perfectly designed for hovering, but their faces were of a different order. We appeared to be closely related yet different, although we were united in our unwavering dedication to God. The beasts aroused in me an unsettled, endangered feeling, but as I observed their total devotion to protecting the Lord, and his complete command over them and ease in their presence, I was no longer afraid.

Moving to and fro with great speed from the throne room and into the firmament were other creatures who looked like variations of myself, some larger, some smaller, some with wings, some without.

A group of these brother beings stared at me intently and whispered. Clearly, these beings were conscious of their own, and others', rank, for they stood in orderly groups in sashes of color designated according to status. The angel bands wondered about what my assignment could be.

I was quite the topic of conversation on my creation day. The Lord let the angels wonder aloud about me. To be truthful, the angels were busybodies—never gossips, no, but they were insatiably curious. Though I was within earshot, and tenderhearted, the angels were animatedly discussing how I had been created the last of their kind by God. Michael, the archangel, explained to them with sensitivity that I must not be made to feel like an afterthought. Michael said God had revealed that he would create me when my mission was ready. The angel bands were placated, then. In a gesture to welcome me into heaven, one called Raphael stepped forward with a leather-bound gift. I felt an affinity at once for the sacred Old Testament.

At the moment the book was placed in my hands, an ember ignited in the well of my spirit, the first spark of a fire that would eventually roar. It was the blaze of a storyteller's gift. Over the eons I have developed a particular fondness for legends and myths and yarns and tales, as well as an acute desire to write some, myself. Since God has given me facility with words—some would say, in fact, an obvious anointment for working with them—I believe it's only right that I respond and use the gift as best I can, by writing books to God's glory. My output to date is this memoir, but I have plans to write fiction.

Along with the angels, other beings were assembled in the throne room on the day of my creation. They were seated in ornate chairs, and on their brows were simple, delicate crowns of gold. These elder persons were seated in deference below Most High, and when the gazing beasts cried out, they came to lay their crowns at the feet of God. I watched them in astonishment as they processed and prayed in unison. Father God could have required of them anything—any reward, any crown—for they were willing to part with it all, for him. These elders wanted only to love God and be close to him.

As my vision grew accustomed to the light emanating through the throne room, in the distance I saw other beings, too, a multitude more, a great cloud also clad in white robes, each person holding a green and tender branch of palm. In this crowd were persons of many skin tones, male and female. They shouted praises to the Lord in their motley mother tongues, and God understood them all. He had no need for an interpreter, for he had created not only the exotic, divergent masses but also their individual languages. Every prayer was clear to Most High, as well as the motive of every mouth that uttered it. I could sense this.

At God's feet, as a newly created angel and really just a blank papyrus, I discovered that I, too, could speak. "Who am I, Great One?" I asked. I had no memory of living before and no recollection of a past name. I was an empty, supernatural vessel, and I realized I was about to be filled with a purpose that would make me whole. I waited for God to tell me everything I needed to know, even my identity. I yearned to know why I existed, as all youth do. I wanted to be of service, and useful. I know now that not all beings share that impulse, preferring to serve themselves, alone.

Of course, Father God understood my thoughts. He could see them in my mind, my questions swirling there like minnows. "You are my celestial messenger, Gabriel, Strong Man of God, who will stand in my presence," he said. "You will do my bidding to inform humankind as a herald."

I shrank back, embarrassed. "What is humankind?" I asked meekly. I understood virtually nothing. My degree of blankness surprised even the other angels. They fussed among themselves at my ignorance, listening, thinking, as they considered my unusual appointment. A special messenger to Earth had never been needed before for the troublesome human race, they twittered. What was about to happen? Why were humans so unique that they needed a brand new (and unschooled) angel?

A handsome, muscular person with the confident stride of a tradesman stepped toward me, then. On his face he wore a thick, cleft beard, and long, dark hair with a trace of curl in it brushed his vigorous shoulders. He was in simple garb. His hands and feet appeared to be marred in a painful way, but he smiled at me in greeting as if unencumbered by physical traumas. He came close to me and gently ran his fingers over my wings, admiring their texture and examining their detail, and then he looked at my whole form with satisfaction, as a carpenter might appreciate a well-made table.

"Gabriel," the Father said, "this is my Son." The audience of heaven erupted in praise. The noise was ecstatic. There was deafening applause.

I felt different. This person's nearness had an emotional impact upon me. When he drew near, my heart grew light. I could barely contain the joy I felt in his presence. As I basked in my joy, the Son began to glow with the brilliant light of a thousand torches, and his simple clothes transformed into exquisite purple linen embroidered at the hems and cuffs with translucent, sparkling jewels. As I continued to enjoy the warmth of his closeness, this being transformed yet again into a pure, white lamb, and then, incredibly, back into the shimmering personage honored in royal linen. I was mesmerized. My joy was overpowered by awe. I thought I might collapse.

But the Son spoke to me as a friend would. "Gabriel, how does it feel to be a brand-new angel?" he asked kindly. His eyes were afire with luminous immortality, and "the Word made flesh" floated into my mind so naturally that I felt no alarm at the strange phrase's intrusion. "I am Jesus, Gabriel. I am your Lord. Now, try out those new wings I made for you," he encouraged. "I want to see them in action."

"Yes, Lord," I obeyed. Carefully, I placed the wine and bread and book I was holding on the throne room's altar. I wasn't sure what was expected of me. The looming, many-eyed creatures roared so at my approach that I nearly dropped the golden chalice. I glanced at the Son and he gestured to me with calming reassurance. Not an auspicious beginning for me, I'm afraid. My inexperience was showing. So many beings were watching.

And then, ah, then, I had the first flight of my life! My wings unfolded with an articulated spread of the feathers; they expanded into their broad, full width such that I was buoyed aloft; and through nothing more than my wish, I was propelled to the ends of the vast universe and back, to return to the side of Jesus in a column of dazzling, flickering light. My joy pulsed in my chest like a chime. "Hallelujah!" I cried out, breathless.

The Son of Man held out his arms to encircle me. He was so pleased. "Gabriel," he laughed, "what a voice you have! You'll be a fine herald!"

I fell to my knees again in reverence. There was so much to learn. I wanted to know more about my body, which could carry me so. I seemed to be spirit, not solid, though I had been given a kind of structure. With tentative inquiry, I touched my robe and hair and brow to make certain of my substance. Strength animated my arms and legs, though I had no flesh. A jubilant smile formed on my young, earnest face, for I saw that I had been well made, a fact that gave me pleasure. And, of course, my wings! I was so grateful to God for my wings!

"You were created to live from this day forward, Gabriel," Christ explained, watching my explorations. "You'll grow older, but you'll never decline. You'll never marry as people on Earth do, and you will never have children. Those things are not for you. You have been made stronger and a little higher than mankind, for a while, but later my people will be above you."

I wondered if never being a husband were so much a loss. How to tell?

"Over eternity, Gabriel, you'll remain close to me, growing in knowledge and performing my will to help the saints. Your happiness and responsibilities will be found in service to God, forever. You've been sealed for that purpose."

"I'll always be your servant, Lord," I said humbly. "Only never send me away from you."

Michael, the archangel, had a long talk with me about the fallen ones, in much later years. There had been those permanently kept away. They had been cast out. In rebellion, they had been expelled, and Michael had been an eyewitness to the Grand Expulsion.

An eruption of fire carried on a vibrant wind filled the throne room, next. It burned in midair in the sight of all present, roaring, consuming no tree or fuel of any kind, perpetuating itself of its own accord. The high walls shone lustrous with the reflection of the billowing flame, and the leaping, magnificent fire was mirrored on the celestial floor tiles made of smooth, shining glass, spread wide as a sea. The four beasts surrounding Most High became respectfully silent and turned their multitudinous eyes upward, in rapture. Lord Jesus listened intently, too.

"You will bring the news of Christ's imminent coming to Earth," the wind declared above me. My emotions raced at these words. "That will be a proclamation for good, but also a warning, Strong Man of God."

"Acknowledge the Holy Spirit" gently appeared as a phrase in my mind. In an instant, I found that I was filled with many of the answers I needed, and my entire being pulsed with a passionate, irresistible urge to fly. I was being equipped not only spiritually but also emotionally and intellectually for faithful service. Thus, the Spirit equipped me with my personality.

God the Father spoke to me with words that interlaced with my thoughts. "Gabriel," he began patiently, "though you will carry the most important message ever delivered, at this moment you don't understand fully what it means."

"No, sire," I agreed. "But I wish to."

"From me, you will learn the law," the Father said.

"From me, you will learn of God's power," the Spirit enjoined.

"I am eager to learn."

"And from me," the Son said, "you will learn of God's love for mankind and my plans for my bride, the church."

I stayed on my knees, listening.

"It's been a big day for you, Gabriel," the Lord continued warmly. "You were created and called, both at once." Jesus passed by my wings to assume his throne on the Father's right. A cooing white dove descended from out of the ether to alight softly on his shoulder, at which point the flames filling the throne room disappeared.

I kept my head bowed, but I saw.

"We want you to begin as a guardian angel," the Trinity said. "You will go to Earth to protect a child. Come back to us after one year to report on what you have learned. Then, we will determine if you are truly fit to carry our message."

What an assignment for a beginner! I barely knew my own name.

Such was my initial hour as a new holy angel.

I, Gabriel, have loved and served my God ever since.

1

s I write this memoir, I recall that the world in 2015 was perfect for an angel learning to speak with mankind. The year was representative of all that was wrong and all that could be saved. God is the master of the well-struck moment, and he'd chosen this timeframe wisely for my training, because of social media and mass communication. Like Roman roads that linked a sprawling empire, mass media connected people. It was like a road to minds and floated on air. Throughout the year known as 2015, I was to learn about mankind's state of affairs, with much of my new knowledge made available to me on "devices." As the inventor of time, God was not deterred by moving me forward and backward through headwinds and tailwinds of years, in what humans call the past, present, and future. There were lessons in 2015 that the Lord knew were important for my work in Judea. I took as a given that God could whisk me back into history, if I were sufficiently trained in 2015.

According to the Gregorian calendar, it was July in a land called "America" when I arrived. With my assignment came new transportation, because, for a while, my wings were off limits. I alighted invisibly on the concourse in 30th Street Station in Philadelphia, Pennsylvania, next to the elegiac Angel of the Resurrection that depicts my friend, the archangel Michael, carrying a soldier home to the Lord. It touched me deeply to see man's pitiable state so portrayed in bronze, and, looking back, I don't wonder at all why God introduced me to humankind at such a poignant memorial in the City of Brotherly Love.

The "train" station was enormous. Interestingly, it was called by the same word that was used in my spiritual formation to "train" me as a herald. The emerging writer in me noticed this similarity of sound was going to be an issue in learning English, but I decided to save the problem for another day. I examined my surroundings like a young person gone to camp for the summer, and I eagerly took stock of the facilities and provisions.

The station was constructed of fine stone blocks of a faint gray hue, with cavernous spaces that included towering ceilings and rows of windows soaring skyward as in a temple. Entrances were set off by massive Corinthian columns through which travelers could make easy passage. Red, gold, and cream colors highlighted the many indoor architectural touches the mortals referred to as "Art Deco." Several yawning stairwells as deep as caves descended downward to the train tracks. The passenger waiting area was as wide as the plain of Megiddo and was dotted throughout with heavily varnished wooden benches like church pews.

The day I appeared, the concourse was teeming with preoccupied people, their luggage rolling about behind them on wheels to which they were tethered with handheld leashes. Uniformed helpers issued train tickets from dimly lit computer screens protected behind acrylic panels that kept the travelers at arm's length in organized, roped-off queues. Before they endured the chore of standing in line for a ticket, I noticed that many people patronized the assorted purveyors of food and drink that filled bustling stalls around the concourse's perimeter. I had to look in at these shops, of course, to smell the soft pretzels, cheese steaks, cannoli, and coffee. I took it all in. The train station, at least above the tracks, was delightfully fragrant.

There was the matter of shape. God permitted me to choose how I would physically manifest, and in my exuberance I chose thus: as a teenage girl. I let go of angelic invisibility and assumed a human form. It took a few minutes for me to try out the process. I daresay several bystanders went straight to their doctors after seeing first a head and then a foot hanging in midair, while I practiced my technique for looking human. I was starting from scratch, after all. I had to get the feel of the creature.

Immediately, I discovered that mortal flesh is cumbersome and bereft of the gift of flight. When I reduced my stature from twelve feet down to a diminutive five, I felt earthbound and concentrated in skin. Also, the limited nature of human eyesight was a surprise to me. For instance, mortals cannot see into the spiritual realm, and in this lack they suffer from a kind of blindness. The Lord must be keeping human vision limited for a reason, but he did not share it with me. Perhaps Christ does not want mankind too distracted, even frightened, by the other spiritual dimensions in which mortals unknowingly float.

The gift of hearing I found useful, restricted though it was to a certain distance. Later, I learned that even the most common canine surpasses humans in this capacity. The sense of touch was also short of what exists in heaven, for in mortals it does not typically include the power to heal. Still, there were compensations. For example, textiles and wardrobes were interesting. I copied a pair of jeans and a shirt I saw flouncing by, as well as a striped bathing suit I observed in a shop window to wear underneath my other clothes. In short order, I was attired for my first day at work as a babysitter. It felt rather good to be sixteen years old.

Once encased in flesh and covered in clothes, I took a commuter train to the suburbs of Chester County, Pennsylvania. As I climbed aboard, I discovered that God had paid for my trip in advance, since the conductor, Herman Schloss, waved me onboard, having seen me coming. Herman knew God and was happy to help me. He was the very first human person I spoke to, and I do believe he was a mystic. I said nothing to him at all, yet he immediately recognized me as God's servant. One time, in heaven, I asked Herman just how he knew it was me that day. "Oh, that's easy," he answered. "I could see the Lord's light in your eyes."

Over the course of an hour, the train jostled and bumped in an exhilarating way, but the landscape outside my window perplexed me. I stopped munching the pastry I'd brought from the concourse and ceased reveling in the gift of taste to think about the scenery racing by.

What I saw was a shoddy imitation of heaven. Yes, the tall plants with stretching branches were undoubtedly trees, but they lacked the luster of those in the celestial realm. There were flora I could vaguely interpret as flowers, but they, too, were faded copies of those above. The clouds passing by were ragged, the sun shone as with a gritty filter over it, and the dirt itself seemed ashen, depleted of vitality. I was a bit disappointed. Earth looked cheap.

I walked from the suburban stop to my assignment. The Hanson property where I was to study was elegant by human yardsticks. Not quite Eden, but nice. The family's home sat toward the front of a half-acre lot and was a comfortably large, pink-brick house with an imposing red door and black, slatted shutters. The lush lawn was soft with trim, emerald grass, and the front yard rolled slightly downward as on a gentle knoll. Dirt could be pretty, it seemed.

The landscaping was tasteful, well tended, and it revealed that man had not completely lost his green thumb from his garden origins. Woody-stemmed lilacs of pink and white as well as hydrangeas in a sharp shade of blue released their fragrance under the home's first-story windows, and two ornamental pear trees with tight blossoms of creamy beige extended their delicate limbs over the street-side corners of the property. The yard was accented at the driveway with a wrought-iron mailbox in the whimsical shape of a miniature dachshund, whose long, metal tummy could hold a substantial package. This vessel was a way of bringing messages, and it amused me. I heard what was presumably the model for this sculpted box barking loudly somewhere in the yard.

I sneaked a look around. In the back of the house, there was a pool. The Hanson family owned an in-ground pool, with an infinity edge. Very stylish. The sparkling water that filled the pool was overflowing, just like what I would come to know as the pool at the Sheep Gate in Jerusalem, where the sick waited for my angel friend, Raphael, to stir the healing waters. In this memoir, let me make a note about the similarities. They're important.

As at Bethesda, the Hanson pool was shaded by a colonnade with lattice roofing, a "pergola," in architectural terms. There is something comforting about a colonnade. It has the effect of an embrace. Francis, the Catholic pope of the year of my training, must have agreed, for during the time of my visit he created a free facility for the sick inside a lovely, welcoming colonnade near the Vatican in Rome. I learned this fact on what humans call "Internet Radio."

On the day I arrived by train in the Philadelphia suburbs, Jonathan Hanson was turning five years old. I had been sent to be his guardian angel, although his family never suspected my mission. To them, I was only a teenager hired for the afternoon as an extra pair of helping hands for Margaret, Jon's mom, who was hosting neighbors in the Hansons' backyard. The family assumed that I would be leaving at the end of the party, though I knew I would be back, in one shape or another, to stay for a very long time. God had not explained to me where I was to lodge after the party, but I knew I was to remain on-site. Since I had no specific instructions about how to fill my time after the Hansons' house party, I had an idea to practice my shape-shifting skills somewhere secluded, perhaps in their attic, while I waited for further directions.

In the meantime, I was excited by the sensations of my human form. In fact, you could say I was giddy. That was the perfect emotion to match "Debbie's" teenage likeness. My wings and heavenly aura were creatively disguised in the suntanned limbs of the athletic babysitter. Her cheerful temperament and comfortable sandals also agreed with me. I decided to play Debbie's role for all it was worth, and I looked forward to spending time in her robust, young identity.

I rang the Hansons' front doorbell like I'd been doing such things all my life, and the smiling matriarch named Margaret let me in. She was a friendly woman who was glad that her support had arrived.

"Oh, you're here! What took you so long?" Margaret said. "I don't mean to be critical. Every time I turn around, I'm overwhelmed." She wiped her hands clean of thick, grape jelly on a rag she'd brought to the front door, and then she pulled her diamond rings from a pocket on her jeans. After she closed the door with the toe of her shoe, Margaret walked me through her elegant home and past its lovely furnishings on the way to the backyard.

The interior atmosphere reflected this lady's good taste. Chairs amply stuffed for comfort and trimmed with brass nails for effect stood near end tables laden with bowls of fruit. These were Margaret's signature touches, for no other working woman in the neighborhood dared to keep track of the exact moment when fresh oranges went rancid. The mirrors were spotless and polished, the drapes were dust free and hanging in orderly folds, and throw rugs scattered here and there were of coordinating patterns that indicated Mrs. Hanson's careful attention to detail. Burning candles threw wafts of perfume. The silver service on the sideboard gleamed. Margaret didn't seem overwhelmed, to me, assuming that it was she who was responsible for maintaining the house. But I was sixteen and unsure.

Once in the backyard, however, I was speechless. Chaos reigned. I had never seen such a sight. It was half the stands for the Circus Maximus and half the construction site for the Tower of Babel.

"See why I need you."

"Don't be afraid. I'm here to help," I said to Margaret doubtfully, observing the festivities with a raised eyebrow. I had never seen how suburbanites have fun.

Jonathan's birthday party was in full, carnival swing. A theme was at work. The yard was decorated with islands of artificial coconut palms, their plastic fronds melting slightly in the scorching heat. It was hot that July day when I arrived in Clayton, hot as the floor grates of hell.

There was more. A sandbox was inexplicably crammed with toy sailboats representing wrecked vessels on a remote South Seas atoll, I suppose. A chocolate birthday cake in the shape of a raft was sheltered under the pergola's lattice shade. Party favors included firework sparklers on sticks; pointed paper hats drizzled with glitter in ocean aqua; and rescue whistles on loops of string. The prize worth swimming to shore for was Jonathan's birthday present: a shining, bright red go-cart.

In an odd contrast to the party, building, not celebrating, was the theme dominating the lower yard. At the bottom of the backyard slope stood a precarious pile of building materials. At first, I thought that a chariot run was being constructed for Jon's new cart, but no. Margaret had tried her best to keep her remodeling contractors on schedule for concluding well before the birthday party, to no avail. In Margaret's eyes, the birthday party's theme of "Island Castaways" was marred by the jumble of tools, copper tubing, plastic sheeting, crates, boxes, and barrels stored in her yard to remodel her basement. She actually apologized to each guest for the mess, which I thought was a shame.

I looked at it all, outwardly smiling in teenage glee for my employer's benefit, inwardly feeling rather bemused. I didn't mean to feel superior. I wasn't very old, but already I knew the yard and party were only imitations of heaven's banquets. Jonathan's kindergarten chums scampered around the backyard in their dripping swim trunks, jumping in and out of the glistening water and squealing wildly. They were happy boys laughing amid their pool noodles, stopping periodically for popsicles they shared sloppily with the dog, Trixie. Nobody seemed faint from the heat. I continued to look around.

Margaret pulled me from contemplation and put me to work. She and I dispensed sunscreen to all tiny comers, especially upon the birthday boy, Jonathan, who had to be coaxed into standing still long enough to receive it. We scooped ice cream the color of rubies; dried little runny noses with beach towels; and checked for ticks inside rubbery, cotton waistbands. We pulled splinters from fingers; cut the crusts from sandwiches; and poured cold lemonade into glasses adorned with mysterious figures called "Power Rangers." Every now and then, we restored a tipped-over plastic palm tree in a cursory effort to save the Island Castaways theme, which, frankly, the children completely ignored.

At the outset, I was struck by the din of it all. Some cacophonous racket blared from speakers perched on both sides of a blue-and-white awning stretched over a deck that sat above a first-story, screened-in porch. After hearing the music of the heavenly choirs, nothing on Earth will ever impress me. I have a musician's discriminating ear, and the sounds escaping from the "speakers" made them more like "shriekers," which forced me to dismiss earthly music in my first twenty minutes on the Hanson property. Moreover, aside from the musical notes that were tortuous, the lyrics in popular music, when they were not downright profane, were confoundingly, impossibly nonsensical.

"What can you do? The best laid plans," I overheard Margaret say to her friend, Eileen.

"Didn't you tell them in the contract when they had to be done?"

"Well, sure. There was a truckers' strike in Omaha, though, and nothing got delivered on time, and then everybody got behind. Don't look at it. Please. I'm just ignoring it as best I can. I'm so sorry."

"At least the cake tastes great."

By way of contrast, Joe Hanson, Margaret's husband, ignored the whole remodeling project. He and the other fathers at the party appeared to meet in a solemn conference. They stood in a silent, crescent-shaped crowd around the barbecue grill, their collective gaze fixed mutely on chops sizzling over glowing coals. They watched the meat as intently as if they had killed it and dragged it home after a prolonged jungle struggle, and feared that it might yet resurrect and have to be subdued all over again. Tending the children was not a thing on which their consciousness dwelled. Fire was their domain. The fathers stood in a masculine stance watching the flames, drinking and drinking. There was much drinking.

From time to time, Joe Hanson resisted the hypnotic draw of the fire to lift a frayed flyswatter long enough to keep the chops from being spoiled by aggressive gnats. Joe was content, and, after the guest of honor, Jonathan, he was the most important male on the premises. I could discern his rank because he was the one allowed to stand closest to the grill. All others were plebes. It was anthropology in action. Human men sort themselves into hierarchies in this way, I learned.

In upcoming days, I also learned that Joe pursued his business life in a quiet upstairs office that looked out over his home's front lawn. He barely noticed the remodeling at all, except when Margaret was aggravated about it. Joe's other interests took him to the gym, the sports bar, and the bank, places conveniently removed from the noisy construction confusion whenever it forced itself on his awareness.

Actually, Joe had never been totally convinced that they needed to finish their basement, anyway, but since his wife was adamant about her dreams, and because he knew that there would be decidedly fewer lemon pound cakes if he said no to the remodeling, Joe put the project in the family budget as a priority and went back to golf. He had faith in a builder's manly desire to finish a job, while Margaret suspected that nothing would ever get finished if she didn't harp constantly, since progress was dependent on the suspect conscientiousness of contractors.

I stood in contemplation in the Hanson backyard. On my first day on Earth I had walked in my new shoes through Margaret's manicured grass to experience the manufactured bliss of suburbia. Backyards are as close to heaven as many Americans will ever come, and they intend to make the most of them. People settle for what they perceive as their portion of sanctuary, and they feel grateful for it, not knowing how meagre it is, in spiritual terms. Having seen the true heaven, I was saddened by how high suburban mortals aim and how low they land, judging by the Hansons' attempts at cultivating heavily landscaped joy.

After helping to put sunscreen on the children, Margaret instructed me to keep Jonathan afloat in the pool, because he had refused to wear his water wings. Perhaps unreasonably, the Hansons believed Jon to be a delicate child. They considered the pool the only hazard in their backyard, especially if one did not pay special heed to it, and ensuring that the children were safe around the water turned out to be the main reason I had been hired for the afternoon.

I was blowing up Jon's beach ball when Margaret panicked. I saw her stand up abruptly and drop her sun hat. She could not find Hannah. Hannah? Who was Hannah? I had not seen the little girl since coming into the Hanson home. Jonathan was my charge. I had not thought to keep an eye out for the little daughter. I had not thought to guard the seven-year-old sibling as well. No one told me. I repeat, no one had told me.

Margaret flung down her sunglasses and rushed to her husband. "Joe," she said, "where is our daughter? She's not with the rest of the kids." The mom tried to steady her voice. She didn't want to frighten anybody or spoil the party. Margaret looked directly at her husband and pulled his elbow to get his attention.

Joe wasn't alarmed. He poked the coals in the grill. "I don't know, Maggie. I thought she was with you," he said, flipping a pork chop. "Did she go back inside for her doll?" Joe grinned at his buddies. "That kid just loves that doll," he said. "It's falling to pieces."

Then, creation shifted on its axis. For the first time in my young life as an angel, I saw terror in a woman's eyes. Margaret's composure began to crumble. Her voice took on a tremulous quiver, and she reluctantly looked over her shoulder at her home as if it were a strange dwelling hiding secret rooms she had never suspected it contained.

"I was just inside, and she's not there," the mom whimpered to her husband. Overcome, Margaret began to sob. "Where's Hannah? Oh my god, where is Hannah?" Margaret ran to her friends at the picnic table to beg for their help. She spoke in fast, urgent bursts. "Did you see where Hannah went? Would you help me find her? Cindy, get up! Louise, help me find Hannah!"

Joe realized that danger was near, now. He dropped his spatula in the soft grass and walked briskly away from the grill in his flip-flops, up to the deck, where he could see the full span of his yard. He looked frantically at every shrub, at me holding Jon in the pool, at the sandbox, at the go-cart, at the girlfriends, at the guys.

"Turn off that music so we can hear her! Turn off that music!" Joe placed his hands on his hips and surveyed every inch of the backyard through worried eyes. His friends ran to his side. "How can we help? What can we do?" they asked.

When Joe saw the large cardboard box that contained the new refrigerator for the basement, his heart leaped in his chest. The box was open now and pulled askew. It leaned precariously to one side in the spot where the building materials were stored.

After all these years in the service of Christ, I still do not understand the sovereign decisions of the Most High God. *Lord!* I silently prayed. *What should I do?*

Stay in the pool, God said.

Margaret rushed to Joe and gripped her husband's shirt. She followed his gaze to the back of the yard to the appliance box. It leaned slightly to one side, as if pulled. On looking more closely, Margaret saw a beloved doll lying in front of the box, and, with widening eyes, the mother screamed with a power that collapsed the distance between Earth and hell.

"Keep the kids in the water!" Joe yelled, running. "Don't let them come out of the water!"

The children began to wail. I held Jonathan as he trembled.

"Hank! Greg!" Joe called. "Stan, keep Maggie back! Debbie, do not let go of my son!"

"Joe, what's Hannah's doll doing down there? She never leaves Betsy lying around," Margaret sobbed. She fought with her fists to shove off Stan's strong grip.

The men ran to the box. Joe fell to his knees. He pulled gingerly on the corrugated board, aghast, opening the refrigerator's door slowly, and his beautiful, suffocated daughter tumbled into his arms. "No, no! Hannah!" he shouted. "Oh, God, no, oh, God, no!"

Joe clutched his little girl tightly inside his arms, stroking her auburn hair, wracked with anguish.

"Sissy!" Jonathan screamed from the pool. He evaded my grasp for a moment, slapping my face, scratching my arms with his frenzied hands, but I recovered my hold on the boy. In his flailing, he scraped his forehead deeply on the pool's rough edge. Jon was silent after that blow, mute as a swan and ashen as a mourning dove. Scarlet drops of his lifeblood trickled onto the pool's cold waters. I pulled little Jon to my heart and held him close, but a neighbor scooped him from me. Another neighbor followed quickly behind, carrying Jon's dog. Margaret had fainted from grief, and her friends sought to revive her, all the while coping with their own pierced emotions and wondering how to protect their traumatized children from the tragedy. Finally, they wrapped Margaret gently in a beach towel as the only gesture of comfort they could think up, under the circumstances, and gathered their own children to take them indoors.

One of these women called for an ambulance. The group of partygoers rolled back like the sea as Hannah was removed from the yard. Joe would not let go of his daughter, and he could not rise from his knees. His friends placed their hands under his arms and guided him into the ambulance to accompany Hannah. A wheelchair was unfolded for Margaret, and she disappeared into a waiting van.

The backyard was suddenly silent. I crawled out of the water, in shock myself, and forgotten by the family who had hired me. I stood soaking wet and completely alone.

There was only one thing to do.

Like an injured child, I went home for help.

2

There is no way to tell this story without tears.

I flew straight back to heaven with an urgent entreaty: Why? In a single afternoon on Earth, I had seen one child's life celebrated and another child's life extinguished. Why does a particular child live and another die? Why hadn't the forces for good in God's world cried out the danger when Hannah crawled into the refrigerator, playing house like her mother Margaret with her basement project? Why had other holy angels not pressed a protective hand to stop a lock from latching? Why had they not curled up inside the appliance with the girl to breathe heavenly respiration into those soft, pink lips until help arrived?

I had never expected to witness tragedy. The word wasn't yet in my vocabulary. I thought I could be a positive influence as a guardian, useful in reminding a boy to brush his teeth at bedtime and not to go to sleep with wet hair. I was little more than a child angel, myself. My assignment had looked like a pool party, in the beginning, when really I had been sent down cold to a slaughterhouse.

Imagine how I felt. I didn't know what it meant to be a messenger angel, or why the Lord would need to send one to Earth. I had so little to offer, being so young, and I am not overly modest when I say that I knew how to extend only the most obvious kinds of guardianship, at the start. I had no idea that human life is harrowing, and that even watching it from afar is traumatizing. When I discovered these realities, the fate of vulnerable, mortal creatures rent my mind.

Flesh is so perishable. I saw that human beings stand confidently above ground, occupied with their plans, absorbed in their desires, and in the next moment they are interrupted by whirring chaos, their goals no more than lint brushed off by inexorable fate. Human bodies, thoughts, fond dreams, and ambitions are carried away on stretchers to be dumped in the earth's sunken hollows by those who will, themselves, soon be interrupted. How could this be? The prospect is a horror, a foundation for madness. Clearly, this situation was not of God's doing. I had not known him for long, but I trusted that he worked to make life—not agonizing, inescapable destruction. The creator who had spoken to me so tenderly in the throne room was not a murderer.

The Lord was standing on the crest of a hilltop swaying with oaks when I returned to heaven in my grief-stricken state. His glory illuminated the verdant countryside as the purest sunlight would, only more brightly. A little spring gushed near his feet, swirling in a shallow, winding path over stones worn round, smooth, and glistening. I could smell the sparkling mist rising from the water, and the perfume of the pungent, clumping moss and wildflowers that clustered along the stream. The little spring was a tributary of the Lake of Insight, which stretched into all of heaven, its gentle currents infusing every acre, either above ground to be enjoyed in full view or in a quietly hidden, subterranean passage, present nonetheless.

But these tranquilities did nothing to abate my grief. Though I returned to Christ in my splendidly winged self, the sorrow of my day on Earth made flight nearly impossible. My emotions weighed me down. I felt pale and covered in cinders. I hung my head in despair as if I had been given a new name that shamed me. Although God had not commissioned me to protect the child Hannah, I felt guilty that she had died. I did not know, then, that such is the nature of the world: Whatever one does to try to love and protect, and even if one is occasionally victorious, death will still prevail, always ravenous, and often unannounced.

"Master, I have failed you." I knelt in dejected fatigue, closing my eyes in spiritual pain, not prayer. I was certain I would never amount to anything as an angel.

"Come to me, Gabriel," the Lord whispered.

I spread open my hands at his feet. My upturned, empty palms suggested my lack of understanding. I was at a loss. "I want to come home."

"You were gone for only one day."

"Earth is ruined. Please let me come back to your presence."

"Soon, but not now."

"I don't understand. Why? Why, Lord?"

Jesus looked out over the hilltop with an unwavering gaze. The sky's horizon unfurled in a blue-and-silver palette, like a pearl's patina, but it was only the nearest border of all that God governs. A whispering breeze lifted the fringes of the Lord's tallit, which he gathered around his shoulders in introspection. He was thinking. Jesus was selecting his words carefully, just for me, just the right words.

"Once, I let them choose, Gabriel, when we were in the Garden. What they wanted brought us to this," the Lord said. He parted the blue-tinged clouds so that together we could see, below in Clayton, Hannah's burial in progress. The mourners' wailing filled the hillside's air, and then quickly vanished. Pain wasn't allowed inside heaven. Christ then turned to me to address my grief. "Other angels have brought Hannah into my house, Gabriel. Take comfort. She lives on here. She'll grow up here. The little ones are safe with me."

But I had been on Earth. I had seen humans struggle to find fulfillment in their swimming pools, and their manicured lawns, and their new refrigerators through which they wanted to make a happy home. Humans wanted their time to be alive, at least the Americans did. "You could restore her, Lord. You could raise her up." My voice was hopeful. I felt the kinship of youth with Hannah. In my lack of understanding, I wanted her to have the chance to be young, as I had my chance. I wanted her to feel an exhilarating future unfold, as I had felt the thrill of the first spread of my wings.

"Hannah will never die again," Jesus promised. He then knelt with me and took my hand. "It is enough."

Before my courage failed me, I said one more thing. I had to know. "You could have prevented it, Master. Protecting her was within your power." My words were out of my mouth. I held my breath.

Jesus declined to explain. But he nodded. Many secrets he reserves to himself. He permitted me a great consolation, though. Shortly I heard the cheerful creak of playground swings and children's laughter. The Lord smiled. He listened intently to the joy that he heard. "Hannah is playing with the others."

I paused to reflect on this. "But Margaret and Joe stand in the graveyard."

"Hannah knows and her soul waits for them here."

I considered my earthly assignment dejectedly. Not only had Hannah perished, but young Jonathan, the child specifically in my care, had witnessed her death and had been physically injured in the pool. I realized penitently that the guardian angel's role really must be learned. I felt as powerless as bubbles. Most High was right. I needed special training before I attempted any kind of service for him, much less the grand responsibilities of the herald angel who would announce his coming to Earth.

The Lord arose from the stream's bank and put a consoling arm around my wings as we traversed the quivering, windswept grasses of heaven. As God walked by, every blade and strand recognized and greeted him with "Hello, Lord," or "Good day, sire." Their combined voices created a gentle chorus on the air.

"You have to go back to Earth," Jesus said softly. "You need a year for your training. Gabriel, even more is wrong with mankind than you've learned. Go to your lessons. Be ready to announce my coming."

Oh, I did not want to hear Christ's will for my life. I did not want to be immersed again among the dying. I wanted to stay by God's side, in private conversation, in the gleam and breezes of heaven. I wanted to become acquainted with the other angels. I wanted to sit by the stream and write.

Of course, God knew all this. "Tell me your heart. I'm listening," Christ said.

"I beg to go back on one condition," I replied, impertinent. To think that I, who am merely a heap of ethereal feathers, spoke to the God of the universe with a demand, now makes me shudder. In my youthfulness, I was untoward. As I write this memoir, I quake to recall my bravado. For my insolence, I should have been turned into Martian haze, or comet crumbs, but the Lord was patient with me. In his wisdom, in his forbearance, he knew that it was experience that I needed and that I would learn from, not punishment.

"What's your condition?" Jesus said kindly. "Tell me."

"If it is permitted by you, Lord," I began, "I ask that I never again become a female person. The loss of one of those precious blooms is too great for me to bear." I had been in a female form just long enough to appreciate the magnificence of the gender. Losing the girl Hannah and embodying Debbie's female psyche had impacted me. I learned that the feminine way is special. It is one of God's greatest creations.

"Very well," Jesus said. "You have my blessing."

Nothing more remained to be said. I had confessed my pain and confusion, and I had been given direction by God. I dared say no more. I am only a courier. I know my place.

Today, I write in this book as a creature with thousands of years of awareness. I go to the tulip fields of heaven to visit with Hannah often. Now, she is my friend. She has grown into a lovely, wise woman, for her soul matured in paradise. Hannah feels no loss for her early demise because she is with God. When I stop by to visit, she anoints me with oils pressed from the tulips, and all of my turbulent memories of the day of her death are calmed.

3

I returned to the proving ground of Clayton, Pennsylvania, as a young angel refined by heartbreak. I had seen human death and learned that even it is under God's control. Jesus, himself, had reassured me. Jesus, himself, planned to resolve the fate of mankind. My part was to learn enough in the field to announce God's strategy, the details of which I did not know at the time. But my heart was willing to continue my somber mission.

As I flew back to Earth through the shining firmament, I assumed the figure of an elderly man I called "Dave Kryzinsky." I was inspired to assume that identity as I winged over Poland, for in flying over the nation I remembered the warm babka I'd enjoyed on the train on my first trip to Clayton. I suppose I was looking for comfort food, and in my prior babysitter state, I'd discovered a preference for Eastern European pastries. Dave rather looked like a doughy, yeasty babka, with his fleshy stomach and rounded arms and legs. I also gave him mysterious Slavic eyes as dark as currants and a thick mat of white hair above two large, prominent ears.

My affinity for pastry was an indulgence I allowed in myself. I see now that already I was developing the human tendency to justify the satisfying of a potentially impure appetite, and that impulse arose in me as a direct result of my time on a fallen, corrupting planet. In a human form, I found it easy to find a good reason to do whatever

I wanted, mainly by contrasting in my mind what I indulged in with the many pleasures I sanctimoniously abstained from. For instance, I allowed myself to wolf down pastry because I didn't drink vodka martinis or drive sports cars too fast or shop for custom-made shirts like there is no tomorrow. In truth, I might have eventually succumbed to those excesses, and that is probably part of the reason why God limited my time on Earth to no more than one year. Any longer and it might have been impossible for me to get back into heaven. I might have become accustomed to the polluted desires of a broken, sullied world and no longer yearned for or appreciated holiness. My intended inoculation from sin would've become a full-blown case of it, acquired through contagion.

Thus, when returning to Earth I ate goodies and hoped my appetites could be disciplined away from gluttony inside the constraining fellowship of mealtimes with my family, the Hansons. Unbeknownst to the family, I was counting on them for a lot. They would help me not to overeat. I should have turned to God in a request for more self-discipline. After all, it was I who was supposed to be protecting the Hansons, especially Jon, and not vice versa.

After I came home to heaven at the conclusion of my mission, I made my peace with sugar. The Lord smelled my breath and had to work a cure in me. Today, bakers of every stripe are special in my eyes, but I don't over-indulge in eating their wares. Sometimes, my good friend Bishop Honoré, the bakers' patron saint, and I make secret visits to their ovens or even lick their batter spoons. Saint Honoré and I review the bakers' recipes in a clandestine critique and then mystically inspire them with improvements. Don't worry. We don't bring any germs to the kitchens. None exist where we come from.

As the humans say, it's the small things that matter. I believe the Lord invented petite pick-me-ups such as pastries with a hot cup of tea and a slice of lemon. Fallen humans had to be granted something to help them through their spiritually quarantined hours. While I am always amazed at the unwinding gorgeousness of the Milky Way, for example, I have also come to be so thankful for the humble alchemy of combining a handful of yeast, warm water, soft flour, and a big, fresh egg. Though these ingredients do not produce a galaxy, their mixture results in a glory that appears so simple but which is quite profound in its ability to instill serenity. Baking brings not only nourishment but also joy, even a kind of redemption of fire, when heat is put to uplifting use in making pastry, not damnation. As with so many delights, moderation in consumption is the key.

Like me, the humans enjoy their food, too, often to such a degree as to cause them harm. At least, that was my initial interpretation concerning the narrative about Eve in the Scriptures. When I first read that story in the Old Testament, I couldn't understand what all of the fuss was about. I thought here is a baker in the making, a cook reaching out into her garden for the freshest, most succulent fruit she could find on that particular day. After reading the chapters, I felt instant kinship with Eve and wondered if she had gone with Stayman or Granny Smith. Alas, no. After a second, more careful reading, I learned this first woman's problem was not a gourmand's preference for fresh apples instead of frozen raspberries.

Eve's downfall was her lack of a willingness to enjoy and be content with those pleasures the Lord permits, which demonstrates a shortcoming in her faith, in my view, not in her culinary prowess. She was struggling with the question of why the Lord sometimes creates that which must not be imbibed. According to God's decree, apples were not on the menu, though they hung in resplendent abundance and time-saving convenience on a nearby tree, just ripe for picking. The logic of decorating a garden with forbidden fruit is baffling, granted. But God's ways are not man's ways.

Still, Mrs. Adam was very young when she transgressed, in a time of her life when temptations are so vibrantly red and intoxicatingly appetizing—and consequences, so pale and bland. I, too, know what can happen when one is young. And, to be fair, Adam was no help at all. It seems to have been possible to simply lead him around by the nose, though I would never say that in front of God. What a pair! It's extraordinary that the unhelpful, lying snake in the story didn't eat them both.

But back to Dave Kryzinsky. Some people have commented that he was an interesting choice for me. In selecting an older form for my second trip to Earth, I took on the arthritic aches and bursitis gripes so common in a person who has lived a long life, by earthly measures. I felt that state was important for me to experience, for it brought me more understanding of man's plight, my main goal. I feared I would not be well educated if I had dwelt on Earth solely in the comfortable, warm blood and smooth skin of a youth.

Alas, I came to sense that I had imprisoned myself. The prison of old age, mortals well know, is inescapable. For most, old age is a fortress of decline surrounded by a moat of dejected acceptance. Every person endures an execution on the site's cold bricks, unless they are felled early in their life by yet another miserable human fate such as injury or illness.

These realizations almost sent me back to heaven, once again in great despair and on my knees. Let me simply say this: I thank God that I am not solid, for my angelic state is a spirit. In writing this memoir, I give human flesh credit for getting out of bed every day. What mortals live with, and what awaits them, is ghastly. Until I bore the skin of Dave Kryzinsky, I had no inkling of what it means to face the challenges that come when one's human body no longer obeys one's will due to old age. Moreover, I hadn't a clue about the bravery that is required when one's mind becomes dim, shrouding even one's core self like a wraith lost in a fog. Through Dave's advanced age, I learned just how far the Lord's original masterpiece of human beings had fallen, as a consequence of the terrible separation described in Genesis.

Full of the cares of old age, I went back to Pennsylvania independently, for I knew the way, now, and did not need to be guided on train tracks. I did not go directly to Jonathan's house, for I would not be expected there, as before. Clayton had not changed since I'd been away, except that July had receded for August. The Lord's demarcation of months was established in the moon and the stars, and I found his summer times quite humid in the land of my assignment. I was grateful that I'd been commissioned during the era of air-conditioning. I felt human perspirations profusely.

So, there I was, back on terra firma as Dave. I made my way into the city's center, to Grandfield Park, but was enticed to make just one quick stop before resuming my mission as an angel in training. Of all the emotions I might have felt when I returned to Earth, I was seized with a desire to play the trumpet. Making music is a part of who I am. My sorrow for the Hanson family eased when I imagined writing songs. In music, I found a retreat and a respite for a while from the cares of the world. I did not have to be on Earth very long at all before my angelic nature was nearly overcome by humanity's burdens and aberrant desires, and music helped me to survive.

I found a gleaming instrument at the local music store, which was just off the public square, next to a sporting goods shop. When I, that is, Dave, forgot that I had no way to pay for the trumpet, I discovered to my delight that it had been paid for in advance by a "benevolent donor." The store's management was simply waiting for me to come and get it. My trumpet was tagged with "For Dave," since God knew even the name I would assume. I nearly burst into the "Hallelujah Chorus." The Lord is so thoughtful.

Not everybody was happy about my purchase. On Earth, there is always a heckler. Janice, the thirty-something store clerk, had her doubts about my ability to do anything much with the trumpet, other than hold it wistfully on my ample, pastry-loving lap. Janice thought I was too old to play a trumpet. I saw her disapproval on her face. She was like many people who assume that the elderly are totally inept and devoid of feelings, even. "For your grandson?" she asked skeptically. After all, Janice had heard of the prison of old age, too. She thought she knew where I was headed, and that I wouldn't need any excess luggage while I went there.

"No," I replied calmly, "actually, I'm a virtuoso."

Janice lifted her eyebrows in derision. She pursed her lips sourly into a sarcastic frown and shoved me my new trumpet in its sturdy vinyl case. Then, she moved away from watching me enjoy my gift, preferring to stroll farther down the glass case to another customer, as if she could not stand to see such an outstanding musical instrument wasted on an old man like me. And it was a treasure! Glory to God, that trumpet twinkled and its case had authentic red silk lining. The Lord had got me an extravagant upgrade! Once again, he had foreseen my need and provided for my debt, himself.

I learned an important lesson while I stood at that glass counter in the music store, admiring my personalized, carefully chosen gift from God: Somebody will always think me unworthy of the Lord's best wishes. Somebody will always think that God made a mistake in giving me a life with a red silk lining. In that moment when Janice thought I was too old to be loved or respected, when she sneered that I could not possibly be talented, I learned to ignore people like her by internally insisting that I matter, and that what I feel matters. God bought that magnificent trumpet and its case just for me, an angel on a journey. Together, they enabled me to partake of my musical gifting, and I fully intended to use them to the hilt, in the Lord's service, despite snotty clerks who dismissed me as useless. I hope Janice went tone deaf.

I laugh now when I remember that my priority was making music, even before finding a place to live. I was literally homeless on the day I returned to Pennsylvania. I walked the sweltering streets, leaning on my cane, carrying my new trumpet, wondering where I would rest my bones. My temporal identity was as a seventy-eight-year-old widower, a figment of my imagination that I planned to use to minister to Jonathan—as soon as I could figure out how, exactly, to reinsert myself in his life. Meantime, the old man Dave could not sleep in a tree, I knew, but, even so, I just wandered, loving the feel of the trumpet case's handle in my hand.

Eventually, I sat down on a park bench to think about my journey for a while. I rested my cane by my side and put down my trumpet.

The yellow sunshine warmed my neck pleasantly. The birds sang enthusiastically (though a little sharply) and made me want to write music all the more. My good feelings wouldn't last, however. I was outdoors in the elements, vulnerable, new in town, with no place to lay my head. The lack of shelter intruded into my happy daydreams. *This predicament is going to require a miracle,* I thought, for quickly, night would come.

So I roused myself and did what I was created to do. During joyous times, during uncertain times, I play my trumpet and wait for God to intervene on my behalf. The robust, improvised tones of a song of my own composition glided through the oak trees in the park's broad square, and before I knew it, a crowd had gathered on the sidewalk to listen. "Look at that old guy play jazz," they whispered. It was a diverse group, especially for the suburbs, but it must have included visitors from nearby Philadelphia. A young man from Jamaica stopped by to refine my technique. He smiled at me through his face of glistening black skin and a tangle of heavy dreadlocks.

"Listen, mon, you got to open up your horn case," he said helpfully, taking my satchel off the bench and unfastening it on the sidewalk. "How long you been a street minstrel? Open up and the peoples, they will throw you coin!" He left me with a wave of his hand and a friendly nod. A musical patron immediately approached. "Thank you," I said as donations landed in my case, "God bless you. Thank you so much."

I played my trumpet for the whole afternoon. Stamina filled my chest. *Old age be damned! Let me be an example of a prison escapee!* I thought. Marrieds pulled up their lawn chairs under the oak trees, and they put their babies down on bright-colored quilts to let their little ones nap as they listened to me play. Toes were tapped. Frisbees were tossed. Wine was uncorked. The visitors didn't realize it, but what they were feeling was actually the love of the Lord. It brings contentment, solace, and peace. I, myself, was as happy as a picnic basket.

When I concluded my impromptu concert, everyone cheered, and I discovered that I'd earned enough money for a night's lodging to keep me safe. That has been my experience throughout my long existence as an angel: When I use the gifts I've been given for his service, God always provides for me. My gifts make a room for me.

As dusk gathered, Dave's arthritis kicked up. It was time to find a hostel. *Where shall I spend the night, Lord?* I prayed. *My back pains me.* As I waited for an answer, I noticed an attendant drive up in a van to begin his nightly work of removing trash in the park. Methodically, he went from garbage bin to garbage bin, pulling each overflowing plastic bag from its metal can and inserting a fresh bag with first a sharp shake of the wrapper, and then a deft, sliding motion into the trash can. The attendant was sullen, unshaven. He gave me a blunt rebuke when he got to the bin next to my bench.

"What you still doing here, old man? It's dark. Go on home."

As soon as he finished his sentence, the glaring, outdoor lights turned on in the park.

"Well, at the moment, I'm not quite sure where to go."

"You got to go somewhere. You can't stay on this bench. Now go."

Slowly, I stood and reached for my cane. As I bent over to steady myself, the man took a long, greedy look at the plentiful folded and unfolded money that lay in my trumpet case. He glanced at me warily, with theft on his mind. He licked his lips. I deduced that he would not obey the eighth commandment.

"Don't," was all I said. "Don't. You know not what you do."

The brute pushed me, and I fell on my knees.

"Shut up!" he yelled, brazenly stuffing his pockets with my money.

"I will not turn the other cheek!"

"Shut up before I shut you up with that cane!"

As angels go, I think I am patient. But I am not a saint. I shed the geriatric image of Dave Kryzinsky and assumed my angelic glory in all its glowing splendor. I stretched myself up to my full twelve feet, I spread open my wings with a powerful flourish, and I roared on my trumpet loud enough to wake the dead, which I will do again at the end of time. "Who are you to obstruct the Lord's good will? Who are you to rob a holy angel?"

The thief screamed hysterically and looked up at me with terrified bewilderment. He actually crawled under the bench, trembling in fear. "What's happening? What's happening?" he shrieked.

My wrath rose in retaliation. I had an idea. Adders poured from the thief's pockets, hissing and writhing, as the attendant attempted to crawl away. Every dollar that he'd stolen from me was transformed into a biting snake. The man frantically tore off his pants, shouting in terror. "Snakes! Snakes! I'm bit!" he screamed. In seconds, he was completely naked and sobbing under the park lights. "Make the snakes go away!" he blubbered. "Get away from me, you freak!"

Thievery. Elder abuse. These were new, repulsive things to me. I left the thief as he cowered, his hips covered with adders, his mouth coated in the dust of the street. He never expressed remorse. He never begged me for forgiveness. It was only through God's grace that the man did not die on the spot. Did he ever repent? I have never met this thief in heaven, so you decide.

Wearily disappointed with human nature, I assumed the form of old Dave once again and picked up my trumpet case. My beautiful day in the sun was ruined. Was my every experience on Earth to be spoiled? The Lord had provided enough money for a night in a hostel through my music, but in defending my human form, my dollars had slithered away. I looked into the sky. The night air was heavy now, and I had no place to sleep. Not knowing what else to do, simply trusting that God was with me, I walked to the only building I saw shining in the darkened town square. I was wise to choose it. It was like a wonderful, heavenly portal.

It was Clayton's public library. I walked in, immaterial, right through the walls. Let us rejoice! The place was full of books! They lined shelves from floor to ceiling. What an incredible place to discover, a preserve for masterpieces. Besides babka, humanity has been given another comfort in interesting reading materials. To this day, I thank the Lord for the gift of books. The Holy Spirit is an author, and he has shared himself through imparting a skill with words that sparkles like a flame in people known as writers.

Once in the library, I chose a spot illuminated by a bright floor lamp, since I, traveling incognito, could not use my golden halo for light. I sat down heavily with my trumpet and cane. I slipped off my shoes. The upper room was cool in the summer heat, and my chair at a table just fit my form. I took a deep, exhausted breath. I inhaled the luscious scent of papery pages that true writers adore. Though I as an angel do not need any rest, Dave's body did, and I slept with my head on a copy of Mark Twain's *Letters from the Earth* that someone with very fine literary taste had been enjoying. Recently, I asked Sam Clemens about that incendiary little book, and he said, well, he was in a bad mood when he wrote it.

Since that night, my first visit to the refuge known as a town library, I have always found relief in the company of manuscripts. I pray that this memoir I'm composing now will one day be a worthwhile addition to heaven's celestial literature and that it might survive the fire that will lead to the New Earth. I want to tell my story, and I want to make my music. Both were given to me by God.

In the morning in Clayton, I awoke preoccupied with my responsibilities.

I had to find Jonathan.

4

In my training on Earth, the Lord's guidance never looked like what I expected. He always surprised me. I never doubt that the Lord will act on my behalf, but I am constantly amazed by how his help appears. Divine direction is never provided the same way twice, for Most High never runs out of variations on a theme. God is immensely creative! Whenever I recognize his approach or become familiar with what might be called his technique, he recasts the clay, and once again I am left in awe of his inexhaustible creativity. Countless times he has left me breathless in admiration of him.

No, I was not a spiritual doubter when I opened my sleepy eyes in the library of Clayton, Pennsylvania. Still, it took me a moment to recognize a bona fide act of divine intervention, for I was awakened at the library table by none other than Margaret Hanson, Jonathan's mother, who was in her own state of amazement because of my presence in a locked building. Margaret was dumbfounded as to how I had entered the premises without setting off alarms that would have awakened half of Clayton, normally.

I deduced that the Spirit had drawn me to Margaret's place of employment, salvaging my loss of a night's rest in a hotel by providing other accommodations, unusual though they were, and expertly turning my misfortune in the park into a point of entry into Jonathan's life. This event helped me to learn to follow the

Lord's lead. I was young in my ability to follow him, and he often got ahead of me. Since that morning in Clayton, I have discovered that God can put me into all sorts of situations, and it is best to just wake up and pray about them, regardless.

On her end, Margaret had no earthly idea why an elderly man should be found snoring on the mezzanine of the library in defiance of expensive security systems, and when the sun was barely up. If she had lacked the curiosity that I came to know so well, Margaret would have never come near me. A dim, unimaginative Margaret would have been content to ascribe a geriatric cat burglar to a malfunctioning keyhole and would've called the building's security without contemplating the odd interloper with any scrutiny whatsoever. Not my Margaret. Instead, she came to stand over me in wonderment, as if she were seeing a genie out of a bottle. She just had to know who I was and how I'd gotten in. She had to have me *explained*, and her bravery and intellect thrust her forward to my study table for answers.

The Lord's intervention does that: It makes people slack-jawed. I want to make one thing clear in this memoir: God is never diverted. Though he had intended for me to pay for my room by playing my horn, the Lord reorganized his approach without so much as a pause when a thief temporarily confounded his will. Dave's body was sheltered within a library's walls instead of a hotel's, and my training continued like nothing had happened. Do not ever try to circumvent God's plans. He simply picks up at the juncture of complication and redesigns the circumstances to fulfill his original goals, never missing a beat. The Lord might have initially planned for me to meet Margaret at a Chinese food truck outside my hotel, but that didn't matter. I did reunite with Margaret Hanson, and the thief got pants full of snakes.

Of course, Mrs. Hanson did not know that she was part of a divine plan. Gingerly, she tapped my shoulder, half fearing that I was a murderous felon about to rip out her eyes, and half fearing I was an unfortunate Alzheimer's patient inconveniently dead on her watch. How could she say, and without the dangerous act of tapping my arm?

How courageous she was, especially when motivated by curiosity. She is still like that. Sometime I will tell you of her skydiving skills.

"Excuse me, sir. Are you breathing?" Margaret had asked, peering down at me sleeping on my table. "Are you all right? You haven't been here for the whole night, have you? Sir?"

I sat up groggily and smiled at Margaret. The last time I had seen her was on the worst day of her life. She was pale still but able to function. She was well enough now to go back to her job as a library volunteer. I wanted to take Margaret by both hands and say, "Oh, Maggie, Hannah is fine! Wait till you see her!" Naturally, I could not. Instead, I was subdued. Like an actor, I began the long scene of a play that would make up my interactions with Margaret and her family, until God would reveal my real nature to them in heaven in his good time. "Oh, hello. I'm all right," I said. "Yes, I'm fine. I've just been enjoying the American Literature section." Denzel Washington could not have performed any better.

"It's six o'clock in the morning. I'm supposed to be the first one here."

"Don't be afraid. I'm sorry if I frightened you. I must have dozed off."

"When? Last night? Chuck Jones locked the library at midnight." Margaret looked at me closely. She was perplexed. I made my own observations. I saw that Margaret was carrying a book she'd checked out for herself: *Grieving the Loss of Your Child*. She saw me reading the book's spine and tucked the volume under her arm so I wouldn't stare. "Can I call anybody for you, sir? What did you say your name was?"

"Dave Kryzinsky."

"Good morning, Mr. Kryzinsky. I'm Margaret Hanson." She extended her hand.

I resisted the urge to say "I know."

"You can call me Dave," I replied.

Margaret looked around the room nervously. She was making a final decision about whether or not I was a burglar. "Well, Dave, if you need it, the men's room is over there, around the stacks. And there's a coffee shop across the street." Instead of giving me the burglar's title, Margaret was assuming that I was simply misplaced.

"Thank you. All of those things will come in handy."

Margaret fiddled with the security tag she wore on a string around her neck. She made small talk. She was aching to know more. "Is this your instrument?"

"Yes. It's a trumpet. I take it everywhere." I stood up and rubbed my back. It was stiff. I hate human backs.

Margaret, still off balance, wondered how to proceed with me. "Should you be anywhere, Dave? Are you on a schedule? What do you do for a living?"

At this point, only one earthly profession was at the top of my mind, and my knees still ached in the recollection. "Oh, I'm a garbage man," I said. "I'm retired from waste management." The thief had made a lasting impression on me.

"I see, I see. That's good. Waste management is good." Margaret pushed a strand of long brown hair behind an ear. She'd run out of words. She took to fidgeting in the silence, and it was all she could do to keep from blurting, "How the heck did you get in here? Why don't you have a place to sleep?"

I decided to let the poor woman off the hook. "Well, let me be on my way." I gathered my cane and my trumpet, and Margaret walked behind me down the stairs. She went to her spot at the reference desk, and I, once again outdoors in Clayton, Pennsylvania, took up the bench just outside the good-smelling coffee shop and bakery. No matter what I did, I seemed to end up on benches. At least this one was located by a bakery. Margaret watched me for a long time out of the library's tinted, broad windows. I could watch her, too, through occasional glimpses. I could tell she was curious about my fate. She did not know I would not venture far from her side, for the Lord had brought me back to her and, through her, had returned me to my spiritual training.

The sun completed its ascent. God had favored the Earth with the gift of a bright orange corona that morning. While the sun made its rise for the day, I hatched a plan. Protecting Jonathan was my goal, and I used the intellect the Lord had given me to come up with a course of action, reminding myself that sometimes the Lord's guidance is unpredictable. I would doubtless have to think on my feet. Basically, I planned to hang around Margaret's library all day to allow her to become accustomed to the thoughts the Lord would send her about how I needed a home—her home, where Jonathan lived and where my ministry needed to reside.

By now, I was a seasoned street musician, and there was good foot traffic to the bakery so early in the morning. I decided to loiter around there to let my plan unfold. Many mortals like a fresh, hot donut to start their day. The divine spark of God endures in those who enjoy powdered sugar, to which I, myself, was insanely attracted. Yet, the donuts remained to be paid for. There is always something that begs to be paid for, on Earth. I set about making some dough to buy some dough (preferably moist, fragrant, and dripping with chocolate).

My cane I laid under the street bench. I opened my trumpet case and set up shop on the corner. My trumpet and I woke up the pedestrians, who strolled by in a sleepy queue, entering and exiting the bakery. In five minutes, I had earned enough money for a cup of gourmet coffee and had made an astounding discovery: Mortals make a confection for the care and feeding of angels! It's called "angel food cake." How could they possibly have known how to make such a thing? Of course, I had to try it. I cannot stay away from pastries, as I've noted, particularly if they've been handcrafted just for me and my peers.

So, determined to partake of the delicacy, I played another song—an upbeat, happy one to please the masses and make them generous—and in two minutes I had enough money for cake. Back inside the bakery I flew! The whole establishment was a cloud of sugar and cream. Its very air sparkled with sprinkles. The bakery managers had placed little gold-leaf labels on all the merchandise, and workers had hung up welcoming signs written in a pretty script. In addition to cakes for angels, the Paramount Bakery was full of aromatic tidbits of multihued awesomeness, as finely prepared as jewelry, and I had trouble resisting the temptation of gluttony. That sin is so annoying.

To my chagrin, I noticed that Dave was already too substantial in his middle. I appeared to have included a plump flaw in my imagination of him, which can only be expected, since only the Lord perfectly designs human beings. If I hadn't had so many things on my mind at the time, I would have taken the trouble to slim down Dave's form. My goodness, when impersonating a human being I could eat like a horse! I should have imagined Dave as a personal trainer.

As I munched on my cake, noting its soft interior and crisp, brown crust, I watched the Clayton workers heading to their offices downtown. They walked briskly in well-tailored apparel, with small electronic devices pressed to their ears. Few of these people smiled. They were all glum, as if marching to a very large hole in the ground. The lot of them looked unhappy, plagued by the problems of commerce, and self-absorbed. What they needed was music. And more donuts.

I walked back out to the sidewalk. Gradually, others joined the office workers. Students arrived, carrying bulging backpacks and parking bikes in chained, long rows. Delivery men in rusty, screeching trucks brought supplies to the surrounding buildings, everything from fresh fruit for the restaurants to patterned bolts of textured cloth for the upholsterers. Buses smoked by in wafts of violet fumes. Overhead, pigeons squatted on the power wires to preen and coo, and occasionally they sent an unsavory package that landed with a plop on an outraged office worker. Clayton was awake! It fairly hummed. I said my morning prayers silently, gratefully, as the sun shone over the city. This morning, I had a special request. I didn't want to waste any time getting back to Jon.

After my breakfast, I sat down on my bench and played my trumpet again. This time, my fans were gone. Someone in the camera shop grew angrily upset by my trumpet music, and I had to occupy myself in other ways besides playing. "Knock it off, you crazy kook!" a man yelled from his alley. "I can't hear myself think no more!"

So I chased down and then read the crumpled sheets of news-paper blowing about the street. I was waiting for one more chance to talk to Margaret at the end of her workday. To amuse myself, I read the editorials about the mayor's lack of ethics. I reviewed the business section about the city's plans for the nearby landfill. I read the sports page featuring baseball. There was more. On the crafts page, I learned how to crochet a sweater for the upcoming fall. From the gourmet food section, I learned the correct way to chop parsley. Later, I discovered I could have done all of my reading in what they call "online," through one of the devices the workers held to their ears and the pigeons pooped on.

The random sheets of newspaper were edifying and educational, until I came upon the religion section, which was full of so many errors and bald heresies that I tore it into a thousand shreds before cramming it into a wormy garbage bin. While I was at it, since, after all, I was posing as a retired garbage man, I took the opportunity to do field research. I studied the trash can's contents, its material struc-ture, and its strategic location on the end of the bustling city block. I measured the can and weighed it. I pulled refuse from the can and threw it into the gutter to see if anybody would pick it up. I lit the can on fire and watched it smoke and then put it out by making a small, winsome hurricane for that purpose. Time passed. It was two o'clock in the afternoon when I saw Margaret leave the library. I had been waiting for her all day long.

She had to pass by my bench to get to her car. This I knew. And here she came. At first, Margaret averted her eyes from mine, but when I said hello to her, she resolved to confront me.

"I really hate to say this to you, Dave, but if you sleep in the li-brary again, I'll have to report you." Memories of breaking and enter-ing were coming back to Margaret, it seemed. To my mind, anyone who would break into a library to read all night and consequently fell asleep over beloved, classic books is probably someone I would very much like to befriend, but the Clayton authorities disagreed, consid-ering such people hoodlums. Imagine.

I'd planned to practice my persuasion skills in the herald department, but I had no time to make my case with Margaret. So I played everything by ear. "Perhaps if I sleep on this bench, God will cause a bush to grow over me for protection from the summer heat," I joked. "Just like Jonah."

Margaret blinked at me for a moment. She didn't understand the allusion. "I don't know anything about that. But you can't go back to the library." She pulled her car keys from her purse and worried with them fretfully. Her conscience panged her. "I'm sorry I can't help you, Dave," Margaret continued, and she started to say, "You have a good night," but she stopped. She suspected I had nowhere to go. *Could this man be homeless?* Margaret thought.

A police car pulled up to the curb. Its red-and-blue lights flashed magnificently. Surprisingly, the vehicle slowed to a standstill right in front of my street bench. An officer stepped from the car with great aplomb. It was clear he had a message to deliver.

"Is this vagrant bothering you, ma'am?" the policeman asked Margaret. He crooked a thumb at me and pointed. "We had a complaint about some noise this morning. Let's make this guy hit the bricks." The policeman turned to me officiously and tucked a page from his notepad into my shirt pocket. "That's a gift from the judge," he said firmly.

The note was hot in my shirtfront. That was strange.

Margaret's motherly instincts came to my defense. "Hey, now, just a minute. He's not hurting anybody. Why did you ticket him? Can't an elder gentleman enjoy the sunshine?" Remarkably, Margaret began to cover for me. "Now Mr. Kryzinsky," she fudged, "it's time for you to get back to the nursing home. No more sightseeing for you today." Then, Margaret addressed the tall, blond patrolman. "Thanks for your help, Officer, but this gentleman's shuttle will be around for him any minute. He's perfectly harmless. Save your ink and tickets."

Nodding as she stepped away, trying to convince herself as much as the policeman and me, Margaret walked quickly to the nearby underground parking garage, believing she'd done what she could to assist me. She hadn't turned me in for somehow defeating the library's alarm system, and she didn't rat me out for sleeping there all night at taxpayer expense. Plus, she'd objected to an officer of the law questioning my liberty to stand peacefully on a street corner. By anyone's estimate, Margaret had done what she could do.

But what Margaret thought of as my infractions were actually my angelic capabilities. Ironically, she left me in the position of needing to pray contritely for her sin of ignoring Leviticus 19:11 to get me out of a jam with a lie. So I prayed. Sin is not permitted. Not even for a good cause, like protecting a vagrant by calling him a nursing-home patient. What a world, where even feeling compassion can bring mortals to doing wrong things.

As Margaret walked away, I inspected the policeman milling about. He was fishy. His uniform's insignia was especially rich for his rank, for one thing, with winding braids and looping cords more suitable for a circus ringleader than a policeman. He carried no nightstick, no firearm, and no radio. Moreover, he seemed oddly familiar. I tried my best to place him. "You're not from around here, either," I said to the man. "Tell me the truth."

The cop started laughing. "Why didn't you choose to embody a baker?" he said. "Gabriel, you've got chocolate on your teeth!"

I started to smile. Of course!

But at just that second, Margaret drove like a shot out of the garage and pulled up beside my bench, right beside the patrolman. She was frowning. She'd made a hard decision. People often struggle under God's influence, whether or not they recognize it. "Oh, just get in, Dave," Margaret whispered to me. "Don't say a word. I can't let you end up in jail."

My Maggie meant well. She didn't mean to sin by lying. But she turned to the policeman and skillfully fibbed again. "Don't worry, Officer! I'll take this gentleman right back to the home!"

I hurried inside the idling car with my trumpet and cane, and off Margaret and I went in her Honda, without any conversation. I knew she was taking me to *her* home. God is never diverted. For something to do during the awkward silence, I pulled the patrolman's ticket from my pocket and read it:

> *I sent Camiel to you when I heard your request for help this morning. Stay the course, Gabriel. You're doing a good job. Love, God.*

I looked discreetly over my shoulder, but the mighty angel in the squad car had vanished. I was on my own again as a secret helper from heaven, and I would soon return to my charge, Jonathan Hanson.

5

Margaret ushered me into her backyard to wait. "Stay here," she whispered, "while I try to explain this to Joe." She placed a finger over her lips to indicate that I must be very quiet. I nodded. Margaret braced herself with a determined set of her chin and marched indoors.

There was much to look at in my solitude. I walked the yard as if wandering over a spiritual battlefield. The shadows descending as evening came on were shaped like fallen soldiers, the poor wounded scattered around, some lying face up and spread-eagle, and others prostrate on the grass. The invisible combatants were caught up in the ongoing fight between good and evil, and at that moment in time, it appeared to me that the cause of good was taking heavy losses.

I feared happiness would never again be felt by anyone venturing into the Hansons' space. The yard where Hannah had died seemed branded, permanently marked, to anyone with a godly sensitivity. The trappings of mortal existence had deteriorated beyond the state of a suburban backyard in need of maintenance and progressed into the spiritual realm as a symbolic backdrop for dejection and imponderable loss. My young angel's eyes were aggrieved.

The turquoise pool under the graceful pergola was now unused and covered with a thin, brown layer of algae that floated in groups of ointment-like smears. A smell that reeked of dank bones rose from the water. The pergola's fretwork roof was dotted with dead, flaking beetles and wingless flies trapped in the cobwebs of spiders that assembled to hollow them out. Mildew climbed the pergola's turned columns in gray splashes, and the blight had spread to the geraniums that once filled the urns at the column bases with rampant red blooms. These had become desiccated, sickly stems. I looked away from the pool.

The lawn furniture was unraveling, with the chaise and chairs collapsing into piles of plastic ligaments. The barbecue grill was rusted and warped, the fence leaned as if punched by a giant fist, and the basement for which there had been so many eager plans was boarded up on the exterior door. The remodeling was never completed. The building materials that had been stacked near the fence and that had seemed like a portent of wonderful times to come had been carted away, and in their place stood a large square shed. This structure concealed the spot where Hannah had died, and, to my mind, it was an attempt to forget even the dirt where the accident had taken place. One could not redeem the despicable soil, but one could cover it from view.

Whose idea had the shed been, Joe's or Margaret's? People mourn in different ways. Who had had the strength to stand in the yard to oversee the removal of bricks, mortar, hopes for life and joy? Or was it all erased by strangers hired to do the hard work of removing emotional pain while the family covered their eyes indoors? What about the men, probably Amish carpenters from nearby Lancaster, who delivered the shed? Did they understand they were disguising a death scene?

Decay was all around. The blue-and-white canopy over the deck had been torn by the weather and left unrepaired. The speakers I hated for their noise were covered with talcum-like dust. Scattered across the whole unmown yard were plunging holes in the ground, as if someone had moved from place to place on his knees with an awl, digging holes deep enough that light might ascend from the planet's molten core to illuminate the pall spread over the Hansons' lot. Light never broke through anymore, though.

But to my great pleasure, the little dachshund, Trixie, came dashing out onto the deck, down the stairs, around the screen porch, and straight to my feet, where she rolled over to show me her belly and squirmed to be picked up. Even after all this time and in my new form as Dave, this amazing dog recognized me. She gave me a good sniffing and wagged her tail. "Don't you tell!" I said. "Can you keep a secret?"

Despite my reverie with the dachshund in the yard, all hell broke loose in the house. Joe and Margaret quarreled in their kitchen, exchanging barbs that I could hear. Trixie, too. She jumped into my arms and whined as a toaster with its whipping cord sailed aloft by the window.

"You did *what?*" Joe yelled. "You brought home a *street person?*"

"Keep your voice down. He'll hear you."

"He better hear me and get off my property right now!" Joe yanked up the window shade to glare out. He appraised me angrily, his eyebrows bunching together like briars. "And you were so stupid you got inside a car with that guy? Are you out of your mind? You're not bringing some wacko in this house where our only kid sleeps!"

"It's only for a day or two while he gets on his feet."

"When did you get to be so generous? You weren't like that *before.*"

Margaret's voice quavered. "Please, Joe. Don't make me live through it again."

"*Before she died,* all you wanted was to impress everybody with your house and your car and your life of leisure."

"Joe, I didn't know. I couldn't predict the future. I thought if we had a pretty home, we would have a nice life. Is that so wrong? I wanted us to be safe and comfortable. That's all, Joe. That's all I ever wanted. Is that so bad? Isn't that what everybody wants?"

"I don't believe you!"

I heard Margaret state her case. Soon she realized no one would defend her but herself. "Who had too much to drink, Joe? If you want to blame somebody, think about that. Was it all my fault? Don't you deserve some of the blame?"

Joe retorted. "Remember that big, unnecessary fridge you bought for your selfish life? Well, it killed our daughter! So how come you're not selfish now, Maggie? When did you start caring about who lives on the street?"

"I found him sleeping in the library. Then he begged for the whole day on the corner, playing his trumpet. I could see him from the desk." Maggie softened her tone to attempt reconciliation. "He's harmless, honey. Maybe it would make us feel better to help somebody. Maybe I could occupy my thoughts with someone else's problems, do a little good in the world, and I wouldn't have to think so much about that haunted graveyard behind our house!"

Joe let down the window shade with a crash. "They have services for people like him," he muttered. "We're not running a retirement resort. Frankly, Maggie, I'm surprised at you. And after all we've been through. Get out of my way while I go talk to this creep."

I put Trixie down and leaned on my cane.

"Hey, you," Joe said, rushing out of his house and up to me. "Listen, there seems to be some mistake. You can't stay here. Let me give you a ride back to the village. I've got a friend in Medicare, and I'll give him a call. Maybe he can look into your situation. Meantime, here's fifty bucks for you. Trixie, get in the house! That's all I can do, man. I'm sorry. Get in the car."

Lord, are you listening? I prayed.

Let go of your cane, God replied.

Lord, I can't let go of my cane. I will fall.

Let go of your cane.

I did as the Lord commanded and promptly dropped roughly into a heap on Joe's ankles. "I'm so sorry," I said, genuinely flustered. "I lost my footing. Of course, we'll go at once. I understand completely."

Joe stooped to help me get up. I leaned on his arms.

"Dave! Dave, are you all right?" Margaret called from the kitchen window. "Just a minute. I'll be right there!"

As Joe reached for my elbows, my eyes met his. Joe's eyes were underscored by swollen crescents of purple. His interior life shone bleakly through those eyes. I saw sorrow and fear and self-recrimination, all throbbing like bruises in his soul. The man was hurting. He was in emotional agony. And he had no one to tell how much he suffered.

The anguish Joe experienced moved me. "You're a good husband," I said spontaneously. "I know you're a good father, too."

Joe was startled. He stared into my face, wondering. My words seemed to touch him like a balm on the wounds that hurt him the most. This man was consumed with guilt, and he threw it mercilessly at his wife, along with small appliances. He knew he shouldn't do that, and most of the time, he didn't.

"I guess it's a problem, getting old," Joe said softly, helping me up from the grass. "I don't wish it on anybody." He picked up my cane and placed it in my hand.

"It's my back."

Margaret ran to me. "See? Joe, do you see?"

"Why do you have to put me on the spot like this, Maggie?" Joe swallowed harshly. He ran his fingers through his hair, exasperated. "Dave, you've got twenty-four hours! You're free to use our phone to have somebody come and get you. I'm sure we can round up some soup. But the house is off limits. Got it? You can sleep in the shed."

I turned with a start to look at the metal building.

"You can't put my friend in the *shed*," Margaret seethed. "Dave, you can stay in the screen porch. Just stay in the porch, and I'll take care of you. You'll be fine."

Joe was cross again and pointed his finger at me. "Twenty-four hours! That's it!" He went back into his kitchen, slamming the door.

I felt Dave's blood pressure rise in my temples. More deadlines. One day to gain Joe Hanson's favor. One year to learn of man's fallen condition. Truly, I was a wayfarer in a hostile land, and how little I understood of the terrain. But my worst enemy knew it well. He had already invaded my camp. He revealed himself at sunset.

Because I want to record the whole truth in this memoir, I will confess that the first time I met the Angel of Mourning, he gave me pause. He is an ancient, vile spirit opposed to our Lord, and a fallen angel no longer loved by God. When I first encountered this demon, I, myself, was a newly minted, untried guardian angel, and Mourning set me back on my heels. He was a practiced killer, an established fiend. I was just an angelic youth in an old man's body.

At midnight, hours after Margaret had settled me in with a supper of pot roast (not soup) and provided a cot on the screen porch, I heard the lustful, low-register croaking of a fat, male toad. I turned over and sleepily pulled my sheet over my head, thinking that the loud amphibian was one of God's good creatures simply waking up in the night to feed nocturnally as a toad is wont to do.

Just as I was drifting back to sleep with my full, contented stomach and my comfortable pillow, I heard a splash and a thump. I thought I was dreaming, which I'd never experienced before. All in all, I thought the humans could keep it. The dreams were waking me up, or so I thought, and who needs that?

"I know who you are," the toad croaked wickedly. "Gabriel, who has come to protect the boy. And God knows he will need protection."

Instantly, I sat up. I reached for my cane. This was no dream.

"Gabriel," the toad called maliciously. "Gabriel, walk to the pool to Mourning."

I gathered my clothes about me and entered the yard via the squeaky screen door. There on the edge of the pool, in the moonlight, sat a leering, scaled creature enticing me to come near. His red eyes glowed as if fueled by molten hatred.

"How do you know me?" I asked.

"This is our world, for now. We know who walks about."

To my wing-ruffling shock, I realized that Mourning now lived on the bottom of the Hansons' swimming pool, in the form of a poisonous toad, feeding on algae, protected by darkness at night and the sun's glint by day. He had come to the pool when Hannah died, meaning to stay forever. He was comfortable in the clammy oasis.

"What do you want?" I asked.

"To tell you the child Jonathan will die from his grief. Your efforts are useless."

It was a curse. I learned in this terrible moment that evil's weapon of choice is to steal hope from the heart, and I was seized with a righteous anger. I ran to the pool, furiously beating its concrete edge with my cane, seeking to flatten and kill the treacherous toad, determined not to leave the backyard until the demon, relieved of its smirking words, was nothing more than a stinking, webbed skin that would dry up and evaporate under the sun's first light.

I was stopped as I battered.

Gabriel, Gabriel! Father God said to my mind. *No! You are not permitted to take this fallen one's life!*

I released my cane and peered up into the moonlit night. My pulse raced. I do not take a demon's taunting well. *Father, why not? Why not?*

His fate belongs to God! Mourning will be destroyed, but not by you!

My enemy seized the chance to survive. While I prayed, he escaped, plop, plopping away. "You are only one of us! You are nothing more than us!" Mourning lied, slipping back into the pool's bottom with a jump.

I was furious! I knelt by the poolside and over and over thrust my angry fist into the noxious water. It splashed me from head to foot and reeked of death. But the toad eluded me. He was unreachable. I accepted the futility of my efforts. In the future, I would become a shrewd and capable angelic warrior. But for that night, taken unaware and young in my skills, I was defeated.

The dark hours passed as I sat among the weeds in the yard, thinking, fussing with my chipped and dented cane. I knew I would meet the demonic toad again. He was ever-present. A submerged, watery outpost of hell lay just out of my reach. It stood like a stagnant pool of misgiving, right at the Hansons' doorstep, and they never knew.

I was a changed angel after that confrontation. The skirmish with evil was a formative experience for me. I came to understand that Mourning always threatens to spoil the waters of blessing in a mortal's life, and wresting grief from residence requires the Lord Jesus, himself. I saw that the Lord was right. Mortals have more to contend with than I ever knew. Not only are they burdened by their own problems and sins, but they're attacked by the powers of darkness.

For a long time that night, these realizations kept me in deep, somber thought. I didn't want God's world to be in tatters. I didn't want human beings to live under a curse uttered by evil. At the thought of all the perfection now corrupted and in need of redemption, my heart could barely beat within me. It was like a weary moth flailing its wings in a jar. I could understand that the Lord was, indeed, going to have to intervene. But how?

Close to sunrise, I heard Joe chastising Margaret again, upstairs in their bedroom.

"Did you see that? Did you see that old guy beating up our pool? I told you. He's nuts! He's out of here first thing in the morning! I should take him to the bus depot right now. Maybe I should take him over to a homeless shelter."

"But Joe," Margaret replied, "what's going to happen to him?"

"He can go straight to hell, for all I care!"

Little did Joe realize I had just become acquainted with its emissary, and right in his own backyard. If he wanted me to go to hell, I wouldn't have to go far.

I sighed and studied the back of the spacious Hanson home, worrying that Joe and Margaret fought inside it over my presence. My gaze followed the curling ivy on the trellis up to the home's second story, and I was startled to see the boy Jonathan there, peeking out at me from behind the deck rails above the screen porch. His parents' argument had awakened him. In the gathering daylight, I could see just a hint of Jon's glum face. I waved, but the boy drew back.

I returned to my cot for a few hours of rest for Dave's body.

My main mission was about to begin.

6

awn came on schedule. God runs a tight ship. I was awakened gradually, persistently, by music coursing through my thoughts. While in a human form, my mind had used the time of sleep to compose a song, a rollicking melody about saints marching into heaven that I eventually gifted to a worthy mortal for his fame and fortune, one musician to another. I am generous that way. What need have I for copyrights to songs? So dreaming wasn't all bad.

I reached for the trumpet case I'd tucked under my cot on the screen porch, and I blew half a dozen resounding notes without even climbing out from under my sheets. "More on the lyrics later," I whispered, rising first by throwing my left leg free of the sheet, and then amiably sliding my broad bottom up from supine relaxation. The chickadees outdoors chirped riotously. Sunshine filtered through the screening in golden, patterned slants that bounced off the porch's floorboards in every direction like happy laser beams. "What a wondrous morning! Just smell that air! I'm famished for raisin babka!"

While this exhilaration was an invigorating start to my own day, unfortunately the trumpet's blare had caused quite a disruptive commotion in the slumbering Hanson house. The ensuing kerfuffle about noise at daybreak took me off guard, for I, myself, am never outraged by spontaneous blasts of horns, as some people inexplicably are. Indeed, over the ages I have had to learn to pick my moments. This morning, I heard leather bedroom slippers angrily scuff the floor upstairs. Then a bathroom stool tipped over, the accidental target of a sleepy toe. "For crying out loud!" Joe bellowed. "What now?"

"It's just Dave waking up," Maggie responded, "There's no need for turmoil, honey."

How was I to know that mortals put so much emphasis on repose? I, myself, don't need it, except when entrapped in skin. At the time of my visit to Clayton, I did not realize that sleep is the human person's unconscious interlude for contemplating beauty, untangling daylight quandaries, and experiencing private renewal. In a mortal being, deep, restorative sleep can produce unfettered ruminations that come to fruition as works of art, philosophical insights, and problem-solving innovations. As an angel, I would never have guessed that the time humans spend lying down in apparent inactivity is actually a period of great productivity. How clever of the Lord to make one thing look like something else. It's not deceit. It's camouflage. There is a mystery in this.

Most importantly, sleep is the period when man's perception is naturally open to hearing God. No drug-induced hallucinations are relied upon to try to find him. No peyote-fueled fire walking, no artificially created trances are necessary. During normal sleep, it is almost as if the Lord created a state of temporary truce between himself and rebellious mankind, just to make people listen to him. A spiritual disarmament occurs. In sleep, the human mind lays down the defenses it uses to cope with the consequences of the Fall, making a mortal person more receptive to divine communications.

For sleep includes a special feature. While I find them a mixed blessing when I have them in a human form, the Lord loves to speak to mortals during their dreams. He brings guidance for the upcoming day as well as for the distant future through uplifting symbols and sensations, or through disturbing warnings about sin, disobedience, and a broken relationship with him. In dreams, when one is receptive to the Spirit, God often reveals something of himself, his wisdom, and his view of the universe. He might use a childhood memory known only to the particular dreamer, or something mortals call an "archetype," which is a universal symbol that all of mankind recognizes. He might use his still, small voice.

Furthermore, sometimes the Lord sends me to speak on his behalf in a dream. On those occasions, I have been known to take notes in the throne room while receiving my assignment. When I appear to mortals in their sleep in that ambassador's capacity, I am careful to deliver only the message God intends, nothing more, nothing less, good news or bad. I am mindful of decorum, also. No intrusive digestive juices from the dreamer's consumption of pizza are allowed to influence me, and no scandalous erotic fantasies are permitted to overshadow God's nighttime message to a soul. I push those out with an indignant shove and stick to the business of prophecy, as is fitting, when I represent Most High in a dreamer's mind.

For God's children who are eager to learn dream interpretation, the Holy Spirit instructs in how to discern these nighttime images and voices. For instance, many years after my return to heaven, I met Joseph, the son of Jacob and a prominent dreamer in the Old Testament. Joseph freely admitted to me that by himself, he understood nothing about the images that nightly glided through his mind. "Sometimes, I'm afraid to close my eyes," he revealed. "My head fills up with phantoms. God tells me what they mean."

While imprisoned unjustly in ancient Egypt, you'll recall Joseph turned to the Lord for understanding of two of his fellow prisoners' dreams. Joseph had to be taught interpretation, especially since he wasn't a modest boy, what with his unique, multicolored ensemble that made him prone to affectations of superiority. God had to temper his ego. Joseph's explications when the pharaoh came looking for insight have stayed with me, particularly his interpretation of the doomed baker's dream. What a tragedy of the first order for the pastry chef! And what a waste of cake! I shudder at the fate of one who made such fine pomegranate pastries. To be hanged and left on public display, and doubtless while the sugar was scorching!

But that morning when I awoke in Clayton to play my trumpet on the screen porch, Joe Hanson wasn't upstairs developing theories for time travel or inventing new medicines for gout in his rest. He wasn't contemplating anthropology or English sonnets. He was snoring loudly in oblivion, and I woke him up. After that untimely gaffe, I knew that Joe and Margaret would be downstairs soon, probably in a grumble. Their goal was to find another place for me to stay as soon as possible, though I was equally determined to remain in their house in order to fulfill my mission as Jonathan's guardian. I cast about for an excuse to stay. Could I plead my rheumatism, maybe?

As I bent over to tie my shoes, thinking about the short time I had to convince Joe to let me stay, a little figure in Superman pajamas peeked around the porch door. It was Jonathan, hazarding an investigation from the kitchen. He was in bare feet, and drowsy. He was holding a rumpled doll whose green-checked dress and white plastic shoes were soiled. I recognized it as Betsy, Hannah's toy, which had been found in front of the grisly refrigerator on the day she died. My heart sank. Why had someone not removed the wretched relic?

I tried not to show my concern. I sat up and waved. "Good morning! I'm Dave. Your mom and dad allowed me to stay overnight."

Right on cue, I saw Margaret wander groggily toward her kitchen. She rubbed her eyes and smacked her lips. She ran her fingers through her tousled hair, which was demonstrating a stubborn ability to hang in her face, and she stretched out her suntanned arms, her robe's sleeves bunching at her elbows. "Oh, man, is the coffee pot clean?" Margaret yawned. "Did I wash the pot? I can't remember. Whatever!" The miniature dachshund, Trixie, scrambled adroitly between her mom's feet and sat down expectantly at her food bowl.

"What you doing with that horn?" Jon asked.

My attention returned to the boy. "My trumpet goes with me everywhere."

"You woke up Daddy. He's pretty mad."

"I'm sorry. I didn't think it through. What's your name?"

"Jonathan. Jonathan Harold Hanson."

"And who is that you have with you?" I pointed to Betsy. "Should I say good morning to her, too?"

"No," Jonathan replied. "She's dead."

I was dumbstruck. My gift for words vanished. The sunshine in the porch disappeared.

"My sissy is dead, too."

I stood up, startled by the boy's bluntness. This was my anguished, damaged charge, with blue eyes and smooth, brown hair. Jon stated that Hannah was deceased as one might announce matter-of-factly that a vicious storm had blown through, and nothing could be done about it, and it was no use to talk about it. He was resigned. The child clung to the doorknob, swinging back and forth on it, vacantly staring at the ceiling. He was desensitized to loss, for death was his constant playmate.

Lord, what should I do? Before me stands the reason you sent me back to Earth.

Tell a story of hope, Jesus replied.

Hmm. A story of hope in the land of despair. I wasn't feeling very hopeful. Jon was so far past hope that he spoke of his sister's death with numbness, and he was accustomed to carrying near him not playthings but artifacts of death. A new direction was required.

This experience helped me to learn that for mortals, crossroads with God are rarely encountered at some casual, painless juncture. It is often only in the worst times of a person's life that the Lord is remembered, and then only through a nudge from heaven such as my presence exemplified. Jon and I met on the dusty road of death, not in the vibrant path of life. The fork in the road included only two choices. We had to turn in one direction or the other.

So I reached with all of my strength for the light that hope shines, diving into my identity as Dave and pulling from his wise, albeit fictitious, life experience. I would guide Jon to the light. I believe that by assuming Dave's form I was not telling lies, but using, through the sacred gift of imagination, the creative rush of words that a storyteller feels, not a liar. My tale unfolded like an altar cloth. It was good practice for writing this book. "I had a wife who died," I said. "Anne was her name. I miss her very much."

"Did you see her dead body?"

"Yes." The boy's candor continued to alarm me.

"What do you do when you 'member that and can't sleep?"

"I talk to God about it."

"What does he do?"

"He tells me a story to make me feel better."

"Like what?"

"Have you ever heard of a young man named Gideon?"

"Nope." Jonathan took a step into the porch, sticking the dead doll between the screen door and the jamb to prevent any noisy slamming. He was already skilled at not waking up his dad. Jon came to stand right in front of me. So brave! "Who's that Gideon kid?" he asked.

I sat down on the cot once again. I was eye-level with the child. I told what I knew of the Old Testament story, for I was still very immature, myself. Moreover, I had not made the acquaintance yet of the fellow angel in the story. Or had I? My heart suspected the messenger was the Lord Jesus, himself.

"Gideon grew up to be a brave warrior in the Bible. When he was young, the angel of the Lord told him he was a mighty man, but Gideon didn't believe it because he felt so sad and small. He didn't understand why so many bad things had happened to his family, and why God hadn't prevented them."

Jonathan nodded. It sounded like the world of his experience.

"Gideon was so upset, he spent a lot of time hiding from his problems. He wouldn't go out to play or even plant his garden, because he thought that bad things would surely find him and hurt him."

"I go outside. I dug all those holes in the ground with a spoon." Jonathan ran to the screening and pointed to his backyard. "I'm going to get me a bag of seeds and put one in every hole and grow some new sisters."

My eyes filled. Oh, Jonathan, I wanted to say. If only you could see Hannah planting French tulip bulbs in heaven. I knew that someday, he would.

"You know what else? Gideon played a trumpet just like this one, Jon."

"Could I touch it?"

"Yes, you can. How'd you like to learn to play?"

"Ah, I don't know if I can. I'm just a little kid," Jon said shyly.

Clearly, he wanted to play, though. He ran his fingers over the trumpet lovingly. It was then that I noticed little Jonathan was as left-handed as a Benjamite. I encouraged him to give the instrument a great, big blow, which made Jon grin from ear to ear.

Margaret watched intently in the kitchen. She was dabbing her eyes. Just as Joe came bounding downstairs to yell at me for awaking his household so early, Margaret blocked her husband as he landed on the last stair. Her voice was firm. "Joe, if you want to stay married to me," she said, "let Dave stay a while. Look at Jon. I haven't seen him smile like that in weeks. Dave's got him enthralled."

Joe tightened his bathrobe belt. He scowled. "Maggie, listen to me," he said. Pausing, he reconsidered his tone. He knew his union with Maggie was fragile. Joe reshaped his words into a less confrontational register, but they were still serious words. "Are you sure this is safe? Jon's delicate. There's such a thing as too much trust."

"I'll be right here," Margaret said. "I want to listen, too."

"I don't know what's come over you with this...guy. I'm worried about you. He's got some kind of influence over you. We're not even sure who he is, and you've given him our kid and our house."

Margaret poured herself another cup of coffee and then looked pointedly at her husband over the steam. "You can't have it both ways, Joe. You accuse me of being shallow, but you complain when I change."

"I'm just trying to watch out for what's left of my family. You're not the only one who doesn't feel very strong right now."

Maggie stirred her coffee. She was unsympathetic. "Sometimes, we have to go on with the strength that we have."

Joe's unshaven cheeks turned crimson. "Don't lecture me about endurance. You don't know what I carry around inside. You don't know what I see every night in my dreams. She was my daughter, too. At least I don't bring home crazy old hobos because I feel guilty."

Margaret turned away sharply from her husband, abruptly ending their conversation. She walked into her screen porch, leaving Joe and his skepticism without a backward glance. "Hey," she said breezily to Jon and me, "who wants pancakes? You two, come on inside. I'll heat up the griddle."

You *two*, Margaret had said. She ignored her husband.

Feeling excluded and diminished, Joe, who loved chocolate chip pancakes more than anyone, slowly went back upstairs in his robe and slippers. He was downcast at Margaret's unfair rejection and overcome by the ironies in his household. I could hear his thoughts: *I worked for years to make my family better off. I've provided everything for everybody. Now, they shut me out. I don't deserve this. And some stranger will sit at my place at my table.*

This last of Joe's thoughts troubled me as I listened. I had to do something to help the man. I let Jon carry the trumpet indoors while I stealthily slipped Betsy into my storage case and snapped it shut. I would dispose of the doll later, perhaps bury it under the porch. As I went into the kitchen, Margaret handed me a cookbook as nonchalantly as if her marriage weren't crumbling like stale gingersnaps. "What's this?" I asked.

"Open it to the recipe," she said. "Let's get some food cooking in this house."

I looked at the book. I was impressed! Now here was an object that should have brought me immeasurable delight. It was the genius combination of two of my favorite things: reading and cooking. In my hands was a manual for deliciously meeting the primitive impulse of hunger through the application of instructive gastronomic terminology, fully illustrated in appetizing colors near unto those of stained glass cathedral windows, and possibly the greatest culmination of utility serving artistry that man had invented to date. Yet I couldn't enjoy it. Joe's glum face bothered me.

"Don't you think we should invite your husband to breakfast?" I ventured. "I woke him up, and now I feel obligated to look after him."

"Let him stew."

"But he loves you."

Margaret did not reply.

"All right," I said resignedly. "Maybe Joe will smell something good and come back downstairs." If I'd had use of my wings, I would have waved some bacon breeze up to him.

"Find the page with the blueberry stains on it. That's how I make pancakes."

I read off the ingredients to Margaret. She wrapped a daisy apron on right over her robe, knotting the apron in the front in the European manner. Soon, unsalted butter was sizzling on her stovetop grill, foaming in little pools. "What's this big, red blotch on page sixty-two?" I asked. "Did you cut yourself with a hatchet?"

"It's a splash of Sunday gravy," Margaret answered. "My family's Italian. We're direct descendants of the original Romans." Maggie lifted her head with an air of pride as she mixed the batter. "My non-na said she parted her hair with the point of a spear on her wedding day. It was an old ritual she believed would help her give birth to brave sons."

"A spear? Well, that's quite an explanation for being sloppy," I said, avoiding the splattered page. "And did she? Did Nonna have brave boys?"

"I can't say my uncles were brave, but Nonna was. She battled can-cer for eight years before she died. She was the bravest person I ever knew."

"I'm sorry to hear of her illness. I lost my wife to the same dis-ease." I couldn't resist the storyteller's flourish. A tale of my family life was spinning, if I should need it.

"That's partly why losing Hannah was so hard. We already had grief for so long." Margaret stirred her pancake batter methodically. She was thinking. "Today's theme must be warriors, Dave," Margaret observed. "I heard you tell Jonathan that story about Gideon." Maggie glanced at me then, slightly embarrassed at confessing that she'd eavesdropped.

"Many of those Old Testament stories have one thing in common," I said.

"Really? What's that?"

"Even brave people don't like to show their pain." I let my words sink in. I turned a page and looked at Maggie. I kept turning pages in the cookbook, hoping she would see the connection to Joe.

"They're like gladiators in the Colosseum, I guess," Margaret mused. "They know if they show their weakness, they're vulnerable." Margaret spooned batter onto her griddle. It instantly bubbled. "And if they're vulnerable, they die."

"Yes. You're on the right track."

"Dave, so much depends on being invincible."

I closed the cookbook. "Maggie, you know that's not possible, don't you?"

"Are the pancakes done yet, Mama?" Jonathan asked. He'd put my trumpet in a corner to run to pull on Margaret's apron. Jon stuffed his hands into her pockets, twirling his fingers around, hoping a stray piece of candy had made its way inside the fabric's folds. Not this time. Nothing but lint.

"They'll be ready in just a second. It won't be long, sweetie."

I moved to the kitchen table. I scrupulously avoided Joe's chair at the head. I hung my cane on a chair farther down the lineup and sat down. I am only a messenger. I know my place.

Jon smiled at his mom again in anticipation. She sent him off with a scoot. "Go call Daddy," she said. "Tell him I fried bacon. He'll like that." Her words were tender now. That a girl, Margaret.

Jonathan walked all of two steps and then held both hands to cup his mouth. He let out a roar. "Dad!" Jon shouted. "Mommy made pancakes and bacon! Come on down, Dad! Daddy, come and eat! Now, Dad!"

I closed my eyes at the table and silently prayed that the Lord would bless this troubled family. There were so many wounded warriors gathering for breakfast. When I looked up to unfold my napkin, Margaret was carefully adding chocolate chips to her husband's pancakes on the griddle. My hints had taken hold.

I started to spontaneously whistle. I liked the new song I'd written very much.

Jonathan came and climbed on my lap. "What you singing?"

"Just a little marching tune," I replied.

"Could you teach me on the trumpet?"

"Of course!"

Joe joined his family at the head of the kitchen table. He was clean-shaven and calmer now. Margaret wiped her hands on her apron and came to affectionately kiss her husband's forehead. "They're your favorite pancakes," she whispered. "I put aside a big stack with chocolate chips just for you."

Joe's face brightened noticeably. "Can I pour you some juice, Dave?" he asked.

It was a welcoming gesture, and I accepted it. Gratefully, I held out my glass and turned the conversation to a topic other than my presence. I didn't want to drive a wedge. I wanted to fit in, which was not easy for an adolescent angel wearing an elder man's body on a planet in constant turmoil. Plus, I was hungry!

"Margaret, could we discuss an article I read in the newspaper? There's a new play out called *Shout, Republic!* They've written a show about a philosopher named Plato who wanted to ban all storytellers because they're immoral influences on family life. Have you ever heard of this insufferable man?"

"Why, yes," Margaret said with amusement. "I come across his books all the time at the library. Plato is considered a great thinker. Jon, open the maple syrup, please."

"Well, not in my book. How could somebody hate storytellers?" I took an enthusiastic chomp of pancakes and wiped my mouth. "That's the craziest thing I ever heard. What do you think?" I asked. "Joe, your opinion is?"

"I think you read a lot for a homeless man."

"And you sure can eat a lot of pancakes," Jon added, urging me to moderation.

Margaret scolded her husband mildly. "Dave wasn't always homeless, Joe," she said under her breath. "And I did meet him in a library. He likes to read. He's got eclectic tastes." She passed the plate of bacon around.

My literary preferences were in a formative stage. I had to read many more books before I came to understand that Plato might have had something to genuinely worry about, with authors who disregard the public good. Today, in my maturity, when I read for pleasure in heaven's library I often pull out Thomas Aquinas. "There is nothing on this earth more to be prized than true friendship," he wrote. This quotation always reminds me of the fellowship I found during my first meal with the Hansons.

On that day of our breakfast, I let the conversation return to the meal and away from newspaper reviews of popular plays. It was easy to do, because Margaret's blueberry pancakes were so fluffy. Why ruin my appetite by consorting with theater critics?

I sneaked a tidbit of bacon to Trixie under the table.

She'd not blown my cover at all. Good dog!

7

Evil never lets good live in peace for long. I was not surprised when Mourning resurfaced in the swimming pool. Grief is always somewhere nearby. I was at my prayers by my cot on the porch, thanking Most High for the chance to serve him through ministering to the Hansons, when I heard the splash of the demonic frog swimming boldly around in the family's outdoor pool. Though my eyes were closed in worship, my sense of hearing was at work, especially spiritually, and it was supported by my supernatural nose. I could not miss Mourning's sulfurous, brimstone stench.

When the Hanson family was away for the day, the demon had hopped out from the murky waters to assert that he was in power over the place. Joe was on an errand to buy new equipment for the Internet radio program he managed in his home office. Margaret had dressed Jon in shorts for kindergarten and then departed to volunteer at the Clayton Public Library. Mourning thought the pool was his to abuse. The fallen angel chose to swim on the sly, just to enjoy the sense of stealing something from the Hansons and the thrill of violating their property in secret.

The toad's flagrant trespasses were unknown to my family, and that was for the best. As people will, and must, do, the Hansons were trying to move forward in their lives, despite their ever-present bereavement due to Hannah's death. They did not need to know they had been singled out for attack, and that their lurid enemy was obstinately in the entire family's pathway to recovery. The demon lay in spiritual wait for them and intended them harm at every opportunity. Mourning was their collective grief draped in amphibian skin, and he had no intention of ever leaving the Hanson home. The demon purposed to use all of his infernal resources to destroy the whole family, if possible, and if that goal proved outside of his devious reach, at least he would take Jon, the most vulnerable Hanson, or so he believed. But the Hansons were unaware of Mourning's schemes. I, though, growing in my knowledge of the forces arrayed against God, had Mourning's number.

This day, it was Trixie and me, alone in the screen porch. By being left by myself in the house with the dog, I was impressed to consider that I had been given a position of trust by the family. Yet, just in case I was not who I appeared to be as a harmless, elderly street person, the unspoken text between the Hansons and me was that the dachshund was commissioned to call forth the ferocious German genes that were her heritage to run me off, if need be.

By relying implicitly on the dog's judge of character, the Hansons believed that Trixie would stop me dead in my tracks if I were ever tempted to purloin the family silver. They had unquestioning faith in their little canine, as their confidence in me was definitely present but not yet certain. And until I did anything to betray their trust, Margaret greatly appreciated it if I would wash a load of towels and water the plants.

That morning, the Visigoth hound was munching on a cookie. I could not help but notice the situation's irony: I was on a short leash inside the house with a darling guard dog that might actually jump into my lap to snuggle, while unrestrained evil did laps in the pool in celebration of a tragedy. Good was under suspicion and evil was freely amok. Human life is composed of such contradictions. I hope this memoir reflects that fact.

I rose up from my prayers to plan a strike against Mourning. I would not let his impertinence go unchallenged. Trixie lay in a sunbeam that spread warm dust motes over a passionflower vine that climbed up a plastic pole in a ceramic jar next to the screen door. The pup's domed, copper-furred ribs rose and fell, rose and fell, with contented breaths. Once in a while, her sleek black tail swished in excitement at a fresh spot of gooiness in her biscuit. But when I moved toward the door at the smell of the stench of evil, the loyal dog was instantly alert. The Hansons' confidence in their pet was not misplaced. Trixie came to my side as I looked through the shading panels that enclosed the porch. Truly, she was a noble guard, and I was a guard, and I know.

What happened next is difficult for me to write in this book. I was an inexperienced angel and not familiar with a dog's courageous nature, for I had not yet met Adam, who would have been able to explain Trixie's traits to me and who was encouraged by God to name the canines; nor had I met Jacob, who was an expert breeder who might have been able to advise me about what to expect in a dachshund's magnificent character. I regret that I did not know that a fine dog, a heroic dog, will sometimes take defending her family into her own paws.

When the poisonous toad belched a taunt, Trixie was out the door. She was out the door before even I, as an angel, was swift enough to stop her. Something elemental in that tiny hound, who was usually interested mainly in cuddles and slices of cheese, came roaring awake and responded with leonine fierceness in the protective nature that God had imbued her with to guard her family and all that was theirs. She had the heart of a queen.

Trixie ran to defend her yard. She attacked bold of foot like an infantryman, barking wildly, undeterred by the battlefield of punctures in the ground that Jon had dug. Her powerful jaws extended as vises to seize any intruder with a pulverizing bite, and her shining, black tail whipped above her long spine like a battle-flying, Hanson-family standard. Before I could even reach for Dave's cane in pursuit, Trixie had Mourning by the head near the pool. Like me, that dog always had a nose for the spiritual realm.

And she needed reinforcements. *Holy Spirit!* I prayed. *The demon Mourning will be too much for Trixie, and I am not permitted to take the life of another angel! Help us!*

The anguished cry of the dog made me flinch. The tide was turning. Trixie was in trouble. Mourning's poisonous flesh had scalded her mouth. I saw Trixie collapse in pain, rolling over on her side.

"Do you think I am going to be destroyed by a mongrel?" the demon shouted.

Dear, Lord! I begged. *Help us!*

Open the shed's door, the Spirit said. *Move quickly!*

I hurried to the yard and beat open the door with my cane, all the while hearing the croaks and barks above the pounding I gave the shed. In truth, the Lord is a mighty God, and I had no idea what he had in mind for solving the confrontation by using a common metal shed. I knew he could turn the Earth with his hand and topple Mourning off of it into the abyss, if he so desired. But I obeyed the Spirit by continuing to bang on the shed until its door swung wide with a creak.

Against all odds, the brave little dachshund rallied. At first, she only lifted her head. Then I watched in awe as she rolled, jumped up with all four paws planted in a defiant stance, and looked menacingly, through narrowed eyes, long and hard at the demon. Trixie steeled herself for war. She carried herself like an armored vehicle, even a tank ready to plow over Mourning without thinking twice about it. She could've eaten bullets whole, not just biscuits.

Mourning met Trixie's gaze. In broad daylight, the demon's bulbous eyes glowed red, to those who could see them. "Come here, little beast," Mourning taunted. "Come and see how I shall take your hide down to hell for a rug."

I couldn't stand still! But when I attempted to come to Trixie's side, to lend what lame assistance I could, the courageous dog unexpectedly growled *at me*. I got the point: This was her yard and her fight. I stood helplessly by the shed's door, having fulfilled the instructions from the Spirit. It was all up to the dachshund, now.

Mourning hopped in a small half circle a few yards from Trixie. He was gauging her strengths. The evil frog puffed himself to twice his size, turned an alarming shade of sickly yellow to intimidate his enemy, and raised himself up on his spotted, webbed limbs for a better look at the field of conflict.

Trixie Hanson needed no such reconnoiter. She lunged at the frog's broad back, then she withdrew, then she lunged again to try to crush the neck, and withdrew instinctively to avoid the toxins dripping from Mourning's mouth, including the words of a curse the demon spat at her as she found her target on the third salvo and shook, shook, shook Mourning by his slimy, reeking spine. "You shall be blind all your days!" the demon shrieked. "You shall be alone in the night!"

Trixie wasn't convinced and promptly responded by shredding the frog's back leg. Her sharp teeth, penetrating as needles, sank into the demon's smooth, rubbery flesh, and with quick jerks of her jaws, she pulled Mourning's muscular leg into frayed strips of meat. She snarled at the taste of his blood.

But Mourning abandoned his appendage in Trixie's face. Crawling frantically away, the demon screamed out in rage as the dog immediately followed. Trixie ran to remain at a strategically low angle directly above the toad, positioning her jaws for a fatal blow. When the frog crawled to the right, Trixie swerved to block his escape. When Mourning hopped to the left, she boxed him in between her front feet, all the while seeking to pinch his head in her jaws.

Still, Mourning wasn't a demon for nothing. Relying with cunning on the dog's fast gait, he shrewdly stopped moving, sat very still, and Trixie, at a galloping pace, passed over the wicked toad. In a moment of confusion, not seeing her adversary, Trixie turned, sniffed the ground, and swiftly retraced her steps to boldly look the frog squarely in the eyes from point-blank range.

Mourning spat. Poison streamed into Trixie's eyes, and the dachshund staggered with a scream, falling hard onto the pool's concrete edge and once again onto the hip already made sore.

"Come on, Trixie! Get up, girl, get up!" I shouted.

The three-legged frog began to laugh. "This whole family is going to die!" Mourning cackled. "And they're all going to die right here in this backyard!" Mourning was so sure of the fate that awaited the Hansons that he lay down on a large, flat rock to gloat. He convulsed with laughter, distracted, losing the battlefield concentration so essential to victory.

And when he did, Trixie pounced. With her remaining strength, she seized Mourning by the back one last time, wound up her neck as if preparing to pitch a ball, and flung the devilish toad, hard, with a thud, right through the shed's open door. The demon careened off the far metal wall and bounced into a stunned, silent heap.

I raised my cane in the air and shook it madly. "Sound the shofar!" I cried. "Praise the Lord!" I was jubilant! And then, remembering, I had the presence of mind to slam the shed door and lock it tight. Mourning was imprisoned!

But my joy was short-lived. I had no more than sealed Mourning inside the shed when I heard Trixie whimper. I rushed to gather her into my arms. The dog was trembling. "The Lord is with you, valiant warrior," I whispered.

Trixie bore a limp for the rest of her life, for she had wrestled down an angel. As a consequence of her injury, the Hansons never bred her for a litter. I carried Trixie back inside the house and placed her on my lap to comfort her. I knew she would never be the same, but she would survive. Spiritual battles always leave scars. "Don't worry, Trixie," I said as I rocked the hound in my arms. "God will notice your loss."

As I was holding and loving the dog, Joe returned. He was ashen-faced. After he'd gone to pick up equipment for his radio program, he'd been to a doctor's appointment. Joe stepped inside his front door as if he saw nothing material around him, so preoccupied was he. He moved through the kitchen on into the den without any recognition of the familiar homey furnishings that Margaret had installed for his enjoyment.

"Welcome home, Joe," I called. "I'm here on the screen porch with Trixie."

No response.

Joe looked around the den, dazed, vaguely in search of his favorite chair. Finally, he glanced my way. "What's wrong with Trixie?" he said faintly. "Did she step in one of those holes Jon dug up? I knew that was going to happen." Joe sat down. He gripped his fingers together tightly on his knees.

"Trixie will be all right," I called back.

I could see Joe as he began to break down. He wiped tears from his eyes. I placed the dog in her basket gently, covered her with her own plaid blanket, and went indoors. What could be the matter?

"I have a tumor in my neck."

"Oh, no…"

"Dave, I can't believe it. I could die if it spreads. I could lose my voice so I can't support my family. The doctor said he's going to cut it out and give me a big dose of radiation." Joe's world was crashing. I could almost hear the glass shattering. "I just lost my little girl. My wife and son are going to pieces. I can't stand it anymore." The man's shoulders shook. "Just when I thought maybe everything was getting a little better, this has to happen. What did I ever do that was so bad? Why me? Why my family? It's like something's out to get us."

I confess in this memoir, I had no idea how to respond. I was a herald angel, a communications specialist, and yet I could find nothing to say at this critical moment. I realized then that angels do not have omniscience like the Lord. I, too, was in the dark about what God permits and why. The most I could discern was that this man and his family were in peril. I cast about for words of comfort for Joe. "You're young. You'll pull through. Don't worry."

"How can I tell Maggie? What's she going to say?" Joe wiped his nose with his bulky, white hanky. "And how's my son supposed to get over everything he's been through? Jon's so messed up all he does is dig holes in the ground with a teaspoon. His teacher says he's got no friends, he's just, like, numb. Even my little dog's got something wrong with her now. Where does it stop?"

"Have you ever thought about asking for help? From above?"

Joe looked at me skeptically. He opened his mouth to say something contemptuous but thought the better of it. He let out a laugh, so exasperated and exhausted was he. "You mean appeal to God? Your generation relies on that stuff, Dave. Mine just gets up and puts one foot in front of the other. There's no miracle for making the mortgage around here."

"If you don't object, Joe, I'd like to keep you in my prayers. Would that be all right with you?"

"Prayers, better luck, more insurance. I need all the help I can get." Joe folded his hanky and put it away. "If he's up there, God's taken his eye off the ball."

How wrong my friend was. I stepped into my role as an elder person. "Joe, my generation prays for good reasons. But I know what you mean." I sat down on the sofa to abide with Joe Hanson. Together, we would face the unknown. Joe gathered his strength. He had to. He knew that Maggie and Jon would soon return home. A hard conversation about his health remained to be faced. "What's next? Where do we go from here?" I was ready to help in any way I could.

"Well, surgery," Joe said. "They'll cut it out and swing wide of my vocal cords, I hope."

"What about your radio program? Who'll run your business?"

"I haven't had time to think about it yet, Dave."

"What will you do until your voice is strong again?"

"Pray silently for a temporary show host, I guess."

"What does your audience enjoy?"

"Some jazz. Some conversation. Some news."

"Did you say jazz music?"

"Right. That's what I do."

An idea began to form in my young angel's mind, in my trumpet virtuoso's mind. I felt God's planning for this emergency beginning to reveal itself. "Don't you worry, Joe," I reiterated. "You just never know how God will provide."

That evening in the Hanson home, the family felt visited by terror yet again. Maggie looked at the dirty supper dishes for a long, long time. I finally washed them for her. Jon daydreamed of how to dig holes to grow a new father, in addition to a new sister. And Joe held the wounded Trixie on his lap. They were a pitiful congregation.

With the Lord as my witness, I began to grow up that night. Maturity began to quicken my perceptions. I saw that it was essential for me to interact with the human race in all of its frailty, if I were to be useful to God. As each of my friends went upstairs to try to sleep, over every one I invoked the words with which I would later greet mankind in Judea: "Do not be afraid," I said reassuringly. "God is near."

At midnight, as I took my own rest on my cot on the porch, the Lord Jesus spoke to me. I knew just what he meant. There was no need for explanation.

Play, Gabriel, play, Christ whispered into my mind. *Make the news good and make it loud.*

And I did.

8

Thankfully, a surgeon's skill brought physical restoration to Joe Hanson. My friend closed his eyes in a deep sleep and submitted to a healer's work just as Adam had done while Eve was created, and Joe awoke, much like the original man, far better off for the surgeon's efforts. As he adroitly lifted aside Joe's laryngeal nerve, the doctor removed the plum-size tumor that threatened Joe's life and voice.

Joe's family gathered around him to provide affectionate support after his ordeal, and even little Trixie did her part by not barking, though she, also, was recovering. Soon, lab tests confirmed that Joe's cancer had been excised, and only a ridged, pink scar lying just above his collarbone remained to mark the point of entry through which a life-threatening canker of cells had been plucked out. Every day, Joe looked at the scar while he shaved and was grateful for it. Unlike Cain, Joe had been marked for inclusion and restoration to life among the living, not exile that would conclude in certain death.

As for Joe's voice, it was weak but intact after his operation. The evidence of the close call his voice had endured was noticeable for a good, long while in the hoarseness of the delicately vibrating vocal chords on which his words and his livelihood depended. The difference in his voice's timbre was obvious to Joe's ear, for the nuance of notes was his stock in trade. Many months passed before Joe became accustomed finally to his altered voice.

But in the days after his surgery, Joe's illness seemed to metastasize from his neck to his mind. He developed the aspect of one tied to a mountainside to contemplate at seven thousand feet in the air what it would be like to hear the dull snap of the rope that restrained him. In other words, fear had left a rope burn on Joe's psyche. He was thankful for his life and the renewal of his health, but he could not escape the introduction to his perishability that the cancer had provided. Joe was gripped by a new knowledge of his own mortality, and it made him writhe in awareness.

Though the physician had cured Joe with God's help, Joe knew he might have easily come down from his mountaintop unable to talk, or worse. The experience had shaken him, causing a kind of landslide in his confidence. He had trouble sleeping and was haunted by a dream of a flickering candle blown out in a storm. He rummaged through his house at all hours of the night, searching dusty trunks and cluttered drawers for old photographs of his parents. To Maggie's chagrin at his timing, Joe bought not one, not two, but three burial plots next to Hannah's, using funds Maggie would have preferred to keep in their savings account, given the circumstances of her husband's uncertain employment. Joe tried on shoes and sweatshirts from his high school years. He took long walks into the woods at dusk, refusing to answer texts on his phone. Joe grew pale and the ridged scar around his neck hardened into a permanent weal, for worry collared him like a shackle.

I watched all this anxiety for a while and then stepped in. Joe was physically cured but starting to fail nonetheless. So I invented a game. By passing handwritten notes back and forth like school children, Joe and I "discussed" his voice and his future. On paper, he could express what was in his heart without straining his voice. Also, the act of putting words to paper seemed to have the cathartic effect of providing distance from frightening thoughts and their corollary feelings. Troubling thoughts could be tacked to a blank sheet of stationery, left there, and removed from his mind.

Joe had so many unanticipated spiritual questions. All of these were stacked unsteadily on the raw emotions pertaining to Hannah's death. Joe wanted answers. Such a response is often the result of illness in people, and possibly it is the real reason why God permits sickness: to bring mortals to him with their questions. I was more than willing to add my ministrations to Joe's case, to augment those for his son, Jon. How fortunate for Joe Hanson that an angel was already in the neighborhood just when he needed one.

And oh, how I had come to know about the travails of being a human person, sitting there in my aging form as Dave, subject to all manner of physical and emotional sensations. I, too, was going through a time of increasing awareness about what it means to be human. The mortal's condition is a flawed, fleeting one, and even in a person gifted with a very long lifespan, the human presence is never more than a temporary stirring on Earth. This awareness brings consternation when people look at life for the brief tenure that it is. Few do. To his credit, Joe did.

Gradually, the talks I had with Joe turned to his job. After all, before a man goes to heaven, he does have to make a living on Earth. In the simplest terms, Joe and I were fundamentally in the same business: We were messengers. Of course, the message I would carry from God to the world was so important that the Lord believed it required specialized training, which resulted in my mission with the Hansons. By contrast, Joe's messages for his Internet listening audience were nowhere in the same league as mine. I say that without any pride. I must be careful of pride. And yet, I could empathize with Joe Hanson, one messenger to another, about what it would mean to lose one's ability to do what one was created for. A mute messenger? A voiceless herald? Unthinkable! Naturally, Joe was worried about his voice and getting back to work. His work, in this way, was a noble topic for discussion.

So I dedicated myself wholeheartedly to helping Joe as we waited for his broadcaster's voice to heal. Days passed, one into another. Summer was transitioning into fall, encompassing a season of rehabilitation for Joe. I had never before seen the leaves on trees change color. The very concept of such a delight tells me so much about God. The Lord is so thoughtful, so creative, generously providing an uplifting, annual spectacle of hue and texture, year after year. The coming of autumn was a pleasure to watch, and it seemed to me to be a painting taking shape in colors mixed by an exuberant artist. This time of waiting and watching for transformative change both in Joe's recovery and in nature resulted in a type of ripening for me, too. I was growing in my abilities to "watch over."

"When do you plan to go back on the air?" I asked Joe one day. He was tucked under a lightweight blanket on his couch, sipping some soup.

He took his pencil and wrote a reply. "Not for about ten more weeks."

"I want to introduce an idea, Joe, and I want you to just give it some thought, all right?"

"All right. What's up?" came the scribbles.

"Have you ever noticed that trumpet case I carry? I might not look the part, but I'm a jazz musician. I know, I made my living by emptying garbage, but in my heart, I'm a musician. So hear me out. I'd like to offer my services as a temporary host for your program, and someone who can also perform live sets, on air. How does that appeal to you?"

Joe shook his head in disapproval. He reached for his notepad and drew a frown on a face. "No offense, but no," he scribbled under the face.

He's worried you'll wreck his reputation, the Spirit whispered to me. *Change his mind.* Hmm. I had a challenge to overcome, for I knew that Joe needed my support. "Well, what about this. Suppose I audition. Are you afraid of a little jam session? Maybe some improv? A few bebop licks?"

"That's enough, Miles Davis. Thanks, anyway," Joe wrote.

I pulled my trumpet out of its case and warmed up.

Joe was forced to listen. In a few minutes, he was very slightly interested.

"Hey, that's not a bad tone," Joe allowed hoarsely. "Where'd you learn that?"

"I came in the world this way." I kept playing. The music was building.

Joe moved closer, intrigued now. "That's a smooth expression you've got, kind of glorious. Did you play with a band, Dave?" Joe wrote faster and faster.

"Oh, I'm in an ensemble cast. We're sort of known for our sound." It wasn't the moment to brag. Properly speaking, I'm a virtuoso.

I let the music pour out of my inner being for a half an hour. At least, that's how long I think I played. It was like contemplation. I lost track of the time, which is really saying something, from one who was moving forward and backward inside time unhindered.

My audition concluded. Joe scribbled a long note as I packed up my horn. "What about the broadcasting part?" he wrote quizzically. "Can you carry on a conversation with somebody you don't know? All types of people phone in. I'll be right beside you to help with the technical stuff, but can you do news? Some interviews? You've got to be able to communicate."

I chuckled to myself. "I think I'll manage."

Joe stood up and shook my hand enthusiastically. "Let's give it a shot," he whispered faintly. "If I don't do something, I'll lose my business."

It wasn't the most undiluted praise, but I took it as a vote of confidence.

Jonathan came running into the room. His dad gathered him into his arms. "What you guys talking about?" the boy asked. He reached up and touched his father's scar.

"I'm going to help Joe with his business while his voice gets well," I said. "We're going to be working together."

"Can I help, too?"

Joe nodded. "No problem, kiddo," he whispered.

The next morning on Eastern Standard Time, I, Gabriel, debuted as host of "Cool Jazz Notes on the Web." Formally and officially, I put my heralding skills to good use in the service of a friend. I was a natural, though the first few minutes as "Dizzy Kryzinsky" were rocky. "Hark, ahem, hello!" I blurted. After that, I was fine. With Joe keeping the equipment on track and Jonathan sitting close by for moral support, I got through my first show with a somewhat surprised, but seemingly entertained, listening audience. My Louis Armstrong tribute was a real smash!

And Joe could relax and heal. His business was in good hands and, though he didn't realize it, under competent wings, as well.

Once Joe's stitches melted away, Margaret put her researcher's skills to good use. That she would employ her bookish tendencies to help her husband recover was to be expected. But what amused me was that Margaret started with ancient, homegrown remedies her Roman citizen forebears had known. She was careful to make sure that Joe followed his doctor's orders in the spirit and the letter of the law, but she could not be stopped from supplementing their instructions. For example, I came into the kitchen one evening to discover Joe's throat covered in wet fennel leaves.

"Help," his eyes pleaded to me when I saw Joe propped on a stool with a towel draped over his shoulders, his throat covered in fronds. Margaret was busily stripping more from their stalks in the sink. Jonathan was patting them with paper towels and making a pile.

"What have we here? I thought I smelled pesto." I tried to sound nonchalant. "Joe, what a lot of attention you're getting."

Margaret reached into the stack of waiting leaves and caressed her husband's neck with a fresh one. "The Romans did this for sore throats. It's mentioned in my great aunt's diary, but she had to admit they learned it from the Greeks."

"Mommy's helping Daddy get better," Jonathan added. "It's messy!"

"I can see that. Your mother's relatives had all sorts of untidy ideas."

Margaret paused to admire her work and mused as Joe's eyes bugged out. "How's your mythology, Dave? Since you like reading the classics so much, do you remember that Prometheus used a stalk of fennel to bring fire to the humans? That got him tied to a really big rock by the gods."

"Is that so?" *Another poor person strapped to a precipice in fear,* I thought to myself.

"And in the Middle Ages, people tied fennel to their doors so that evil spirits would pass over their homes."

"Oh, I know a better Passover story than that!" I whispered.

"What?" Margaret asked. "Did you say something?"

"Nothing, nothing," I grumbled, changing the subject. "How long do you plan to submit Joe to marinating?"

"Very funny, Dave. I don't know exactly. Aunt Giovanna's diary didn't say."

Joe burst out coughing. "All right, all right, I've been a good sport," he said hoarsely. "I think I'm done now. Thanks, everybody."

"You're better already, Daddy!" Jon beamed.

"Sure," Joe said, peeling fronds from his neck. "I sure am."

Margaret pointed her finger at her husband. "Now don't throw anything out!" she commanded. "I'm making sausage with those leaves!"

Joe and I looked at each other doubtfully. What a treat, we agreed in unspoken unison.

It had been an exciting day. I'd even been introduced to the Internet, and before Joe went to bed I asked him to teach me the basics of doing a Google search. He was happy to oblige. Late into the evening, I explored this thing mankind calls "the web." I wanted to learn all that I could to enhance my ability to communicate with mortals.

While I was at it, I looked up Prometheus in Greek mythology. "Prometheus created man," the story went. I sat back in my chair, in shock. "Well, that's just silly," I said, slamming closed the bright blue computer screen. "Everybody knows God made man from garden mulch."

When Joe checked his audience stats in the morning, I heard a whoop in the den. His listening reach had doubled. "Dave, you're a star!" Joe called with a scratchy voice.

And what did he expect?

Maggie nearly cried her eyelashes off in relief when she saw the numbers. They weren't going to be destitute, after all. She'd also been bound to that cliff in fear.

The Lord had taken what could have caused harm and used it for good.

Who knew that God is a jazz fan?

9

Joe could not use his voice as a broadcaster for a while yet, but he was able-bodied, and he turned his attention to preparing his home for fall. Every year as the cool season came on, clipping, spreading, and gathering chores were central to an attractive lawn, and maintenance inspections were required for reasons of safety. For the Hansons, care of their property was an emphasis they embraced.

Each residence in the neighborhood seemed to have its own weather rituals for beautifying and keeping up with its yard, except for those families who irritatingly didn't. Down the block, one family collected broken machinery to start a snowplow repair business in their driveway. As their contribution, another family undertook a longitudinal study to learn how long it would take for nor'easters to peel the paint off of their house entirely. They planned to publish their results for Sherwin-Williams. These were the sarcastic observations that Joe made while he hosed and shoveled.

I had to laugh at the man. His aggravations signaled that slowly Joe was turning from his grief and dangerous surgery to take part again in the prosaic concerns of normal life, which was a victory for him. I can only guess what the neighbors had thought about the ramshackle state of the Hansons' lot as they grieved the loss of their daughter. Perhaps in a mood of kind forbearance, due to the

Hansons' situation, the other families had refrained from slinging barbs of criticism.

I came to see that such seasonal activities are a typical part of the American suburban experience. I am so glad that no such inconveniences, schedules, and expenses are found in heaven. There, no heating system ever breaks down in a blizzard, and it is not necessary to insure the roof against woodpeckers. In heaven, one never has to call the homeowners' association to complain about noncompliant neighbors, for the community's membership is already tightly screened and law-abiding. Truly, in heaven, it's resort-style living.

In Joe's time of recuperation in Clayton, more was at stake, however, than bagging the leaves and cleaning the chimney. For Joe, preparing for autumn included facing the backyard and the harrowing memories of Hannah's death that it aroused. Jon's population of holes in the dirt made the yard seem even more of a graveyard than Joe already perceived it to be. I noticed that Joe was doing a good job of working on the front yard, but he was scrupulously avoiding the back.

How painful it is to recognize that when trying to cope with grief, practical matters intrude in daily life and require resolution. Unless Joe made preparation for the coming cold weather, the pool would remain uncovered and fill with snow as soon as winter arrived; the deck furniture would rust where it stood; and if not covered with burlap, the lovely azaleas and rhododendrons would perish in ice storms. In Pennsylvania, fall is an early warning system for what winter is about to unleash. The weather has no regard for the hurting. Even though one's personal, inner world is suffering, the outer world and its wintry winds relentlessly demand attention.

And, of course, there was the shed to be dealt with. Joe could no longer avoid looking at the Dutch colonial structure he'd purchased to try to hide the scene of his greatest anguish. The very blades of grass in his yard were infused with Hannah's death, to Joe, and only by literally covering those blades could he stand to remain on his property. Now, in the fall, Joe would have to move around inside the shed, somehow make use of it, and thereby inevitably walk on the exact spot where his daughter had taken her last breath. The shed was not like a marker for sorrow on the side of a highway as seen in a wooden cross strewn with plastic daisies; that memorial is intended to help one remember. The shed was more like a parking garage built to cover a massacre site, a utilitarian attempt to help one forget the calamities that took place on a spot one cannot easily move away from.

The shed was also the prison of Mourning.

So when Joe returned to brave the site of his daughter's death, I went with him. It was in my nature as a guardian to stand by his side. There are some things one ought not do alone. Little did Joe realize I had been there at the time of the horror, as the teenager, Debbie. My knowledge of the tragedy was difficult for me to conceal, since Hannah's death had affected me so deeply, too. But I managed to comport myself as one would who had no previous awareness of the dreadful day. I let the man talk.

"It happened right here," Joe said. He was reverential, as if on sacred ground. "For a few days after she died, I used to come back to look for a hair ribbon or a little sock she might have had on. I wanted just one more reminder of her life."

"You must have been devastated."

"We were having a pool party for Jon's birthday. We had friends and kids over. I was standing at the grill right there."

"Maggie told me a little about that day."

"I didn't think she'd ever get over it. Work at the library helps her."

"How is Jon coping?"

"Just look around," Joe said, pointing to the tattered lawn. "But he's doing better, I guess. Thanks for everything you're doing to help him, Dave. He's crazy about your trumpet."

"I'm happy to help. And let me thank you, for allowing me to be a guest in your home. I think the truth is, we're helping each other."

"And now, in addition to this, I'm a cancer survivor."

"Yes, you are. You are a person who has met great challenges."

"Let me ask you a question," Joe said. He almost whispered his words, so reluctant was he to say them. "In all your years, Dave, did you come up with an answer about why bad things happen? I never expected my life to turn out like this." Joe looked at me searchingly.

It was one of man's most important questions. I felt a responsibility to tell Joe the truth. "I can say from my experience, which isn't as long as you think, I believe God knows why, but, no. No, I don't know why people suffer." Angels are not omniscient, like the Lord.

"I saw Maggie with a Bible yesterday." Joe waited for my reaction. Would I be sanctimonious? His voice was quiet, but not from his surgery. He was pensive. He'd seen his wife of ten years seek something she'd never read before, for help, and he was considering it, too. Honestly, I think Joe felt Margaret had been driven to the Scriptures in order to survive.

I reflected on that. I, myself, was learning the Old Testament, but out of joy, not grief. The Father taught me a chapter at a time as part of my angelic training, tutoring me in free moments such as right before sunrise. I was glad Maggie had been drawn to looking inside the Scriptures, and yet I wished her first experiences with them had been happy ones. The attraction to God's Word, whether we read it because we need hope or have the desire to praise or learn, is a phenomenon I have come to ascribe to the mysteries of the Lord's sovereignty. Many do seek God because of their agony, at least at first.

"She carried the Bible home from the library," Joe continued. "The Red Letter version."

"Instead of the textbooks about losing a child, I suppose. They have their place."

"Better than the classics? Better than mythology?" Joe risked a small, half-hearted smile. He'd seen my Google search history.

"The only truth that means anything is truth from God. I've learned that much since I've been alive. People have been looking for God probably since man first noticed his fingers and toes. Let your wife read."

Joe stepped inside the shed, which was dark as a pit, and ominous. I heard him take a deep breath. He surprised me by sitting down right in the middle. He placed his hand on the hard, metal floor and patted it softly. "How are we supposed to go on without her?"

"Love one another," I replied, stepping into the building behind my friend. I sat down, also, my cane on my lap. "Just love one another."

As soon as Joe walked inside, I'd smelled sulfur. I knew that Mourning was watching.

Then, all Joe's hidden sorrow broke forth. All of Joe's tears, all his rage, all his questions, he poured out unrestrained there in the shed and left them there. He was only a simple man wracked within the four walls afflicted by Mourning. This father said one final, anguished good-bye to his child, who was taken away for a reason he would never understand and which he would resist while he lived. An angel in training listened. I was honored to be allowed into the privacy of such an hour. In the darkness, Joe could not tell, but I cried, too.

At length, when Joe had unburdened his heart, he stood and gave me his hand to lift me up. There was no point in staying. "Let's get out of here, Dave. This place stinks like rotten eggs," he said. "It's reeking. Come on, let's go."

"You can smell that now?" It was a supernatural skill acquired through spiritual sensitivity. Joe was growing in his ability to discern the nearness of evil, an awareness God would use to guide him ever farther from it.

"I didn't notice that stench before. Did it blow in? Anyway, I don't know what happened, Dave, but we're leaving." Joe helped me stand up.

Holy Spirit, thank you for turning a common shed into a tabernacle, I prayed.

When we exited the close confines, we picked up tools and worked as a team in the yard. Though I couldn't do any heavy lifting in my form as elderly Dave, I was able to push the lawn spreader to deposit fertilizer, even if it was like walking over a perforated plane. As I paced the backyard, pushing the spreader and tossing seed by hand in search of good soil, I prayed silently that all the painful, empty holes in Joe's life would be filled up with God. I prayed for Jon. I prayed for Maggie. I prayed for the world.

Margaret came bustling around from the driveway, carrying a bag of groceries. She raised her eyebrows in shock at the sight of us. Her husband was suddenly able to attend to the backyard, after months of staying away from it? The woman was amazed. Margaret wanted to encourage Joe, for she knew the extent of his grief. She recognized that many people would have given up. She was right to admire her husband.

"Honey, I'm so impressed, but don't overdo it! You're still recovering from a surgery," she called. Shifting the groceries onto a hip for more comfort to get a better look, Margaret stood patiently by the screen porch and admired us. "I never saw anything like you two," she said. "You work great together!"

For there I was, technically a homeless man, tending suburban ground with one hand and leaning on my cane with the other. I hope to include a snapshot of this activity as the cover for my memoir, if the Lord likes it, too. It was my mission in a nutshell: I was someone sent from heaven to plant God's presence in the midst of a hurting family. I represented God's love right in the center of all life's dirt and brokenness, and I waited for healing redemption to bloom.

As for Joe, on the surface of things he appeared to be clipping and bagging overgrown weeds, stacking chairs, and tying the pool cover in place for the close of the summer season. In a deeper reality, however, Joe was investing himself in his life again. Slowly, it was becoming worthwhile once more to try to be happy, a feat Joe undertook in the very shadow of death. What courage that required! Often, Joe glanced at the shed while he worked. It seemed to be unfinished business to him. Finally, I could tell what was on his mind.

Joe walked back to the shed and checked the padlock on it, even though the shed was empty (except for a demon.) I thought it was an unusual step but one that was probably related in a subconscious way to failing to lock the refrigerator into which Hannah had crawled.

After that tragedy, everything now must be checked and rechecked for danger. As he released the lock, satisfied that it really was secure, Joe turned to face me with a start. He seemed to be hearing something but wasn't sure what.

"Why have you come to seal me in darkness?" It was Mourning, pining in misery! "Please, please, it's not yet my time! Let me go into the pool!"

"Did you hear something, Dave?" Joe asked, looking around.

Of course, I'd heard Mourning's lament. But could Joe? The cry came on a spiritual wavelength, a shout from a different dimension. I threw another handful of grass seed and ignored the demonic whimpering. I had no desire to tell a lie, but I could be vague on purpose. "What? Hear something? The wind whistles, Joe, oh, the wind…"

"You guys better hurry up and call it a day," Margaret yelled from the kitchen. "We're about to get the last thunderstorm of the summer. Am I the only one who listens to the weather report?" Margaret walked to the screen door, opening it widely. She took a photo on her phone of Joe and me working side by side. "This shot belongs on the cover of a magazine," she called.

Or the cover of a memoir. How did Maggie know?

Soon, the raindrops pelted us, and Joe and I moved inside. The rain fell heavily in a downpour, but it was warm like bathwater and not entirely unpleasant. Joe went upstairs to step into fresh, dry clothes. When I sat down on my cot to towel off my face, I saw little Jonathan all in a lather, hurriedly yanking on his boots and raincoat to go have a frolic in the weather.

"I have to get outside before it stops!" Jon said, wiggling this way and that as Margaret tied his rain hat on. "Mommy, just let me go!"

"Most people want to stay inside where it's dry," I observed.

"Not me! I'm not afraid to get wet! Mommy says I don't have to come in unless the lightning comes."

"There," Margaret said, scooting Jon out the screen door. "Have fun. Play safe." She carried a basket full of folded laundry upstairs to Joe.

"Look at me dance! The rain won't melt me!" the boy exclaimed.

Oh, Jon. You did not know the real danger in your yard.

It is not only the holy angels who are able to impersonate humans.

As I watched from the screen porch, I got a lesson in staying on guard.

Mourning was desperate. He had been out of the frog's watery element for several days, locked inside the shed and recuperating from his fight with Trixie. Without access to the pool's quenching water to cool his amphibian's skin, he would soon be no more. Mourning understood that Satan would not bother to help an average, run-of-the-mill demon toad like himself. Lucifer does not love anyone, much less his minions. Mourning realized he was about to bake alive in the metal shed.

When Jonathan splashed in the puddles that filled his backyard, the sound of the refreshing water was torture for Mourning. To hear the rushing water and yet not be able to immerse himself in it drove the frog to madness. Trapped in the shed, Mourning plotted deceit. His impending demise made the demon bold. He called out to the boy.

"Hi, Jonny, come play! I've been looking for you, little brother." It was Hannah's voice, which Mourning mimicked perfectly! The depth of the cruelty!

Jon immediately stopped in his yellow coat and boots, looking in every direction for Hannah. "Is that you, sissy? Where are you? Where you been?"

"I'm in the shed, Jonny. I can't get out. Bring Daddy's key and open the lock."

Jon paused to consider. "What you doing in there, Hannah?"

"I chased Trixie inside. Then I got stuck."

"Trixie's sick. She's got a hurt leg."

"Bring the key from the toolbox and open the lock. I want to play in the rain with you."

Jonathan untied his hat. He wanted it off to think really hard. The boy stood in the downpour, confused and curious, trying his best to decipher what he was hearing. Children are always spiritually aware. Jon heard Mourning the first instant the frog called out to him. "Why did you leave my birthday party, sissy? Where did you go in that hospital car?"

"Jonny, I miss you so much. Let me out of the shed."

I threw down my towel. From the porch, I could see the boy talking animatedly in the rain, moving closer and closer to the shed. "Jon! Don't go over there!" I called through the screen door. "You'll get hurt!"

"Sissy needs to come home!" the child responded.

Some formative moments in one's life present themselves clearly. This was such a moment for me. I had been sent to Earth to be the guardian angel for Jon. Would I be brave enough, clever enough, to fulfill that role at the time of testing? Was Mourning really too wounded to defend himself? Could I count on Lucifer to ignore the plight of one of his demons, or would he materialize to take me on, himself?

I had to act. I cast off my form as Dave and entered the backyard as Gabriel, the young, inexperienced angel, up against a wily monster older than Earth itself. I had no time to hobble to the shed with a cane. I went to save Jon entirely as Lord Jesus made me, shimmering, towering, and deft with strength. In my winged, fully glowing aura, I leaped into the yard and snatched Jon away from the shed, tenderly covering his eyes with one hand to protect them from my brilliance, and reassuring him as we flew up, up into the rain.

Mourning was outraged. If he had to die in the shed, he was determined to take Jon with him: He would so frighten the child, the boy would never recover. The demon shrieked after us as we flew into the sky. Hannah's voice filled the backyard maniacally: "Jonny, I'm dead! I'm dead with dirt on my face, down in one of those holes you dug up! You'll never see me again!" the frog hissed. Because of Mourning's demonic fury, the shed began to rattle and smoke.

"Don't be afraid," I whispered to Jon. "You're safe with God." I could feel the boy's body tense in my arms. Mourning's words were cutting his mind. Jon fainted against my chest.

Up and up higher I flew with the child, away from the danger, until I saw a sight that thrills me to this day whenever I recall it, which is often.

I saw the whirlwind coming, sent from the Spirit for the Hansons' protection.

It began as a mere swirling puff on the outskirts of Clayton, and before long it gathered cyclonic speed. I watched this wind from hundreds of feet above the rooftops. Round and round and round the wind roared, leaving gyrating debris as it traveled, skipping over the city's dam and the quarry, over the park and the library where I'd reunited with Margaret, and lo and behold, it took clear aim at the shed in the Hansons' backyard.

Mourning heard the wind howling. "Save me, save me, Lucifer!" he wept.

With a flash of lightning and a peal of thunder, the wind began its descent. The rabbits ran to their underground lairs. The birds spread their feathers over their heads in their nests. The rain looped and looped in the air, forming a terrible funnel in a dove-gray sky, and all of a sudden the wind dropped, falling like a Viking's hammer, landing on the top of the evil, smoking shed. The building exploded, its pieces and demon demolished.

Take the child to the porch, the Spirit commanded me. *Hurry!*

In split seconds, I was back in my form as Dave, with Jon asleep in my arms on my cot.

Joe and Margaret raced down from upstairs to find me. Panic widened their eyes. "Thank God, thank God," the mother whispered, taking her son from me to hold him close.

Joe ran into his backyard and stared breathless into the clouds. "Would you just look at this?" he said, incredulous. He picked up a plank of the shed's siding and turned it over for clues. "It looks like a war zone out here! We were only gone five minutes. What happened?"

"A summer storm," Margaret said, cradling her boy. "The last one of the season."

Joe rushed back inside his screen porch, the door slamming behind him. He frantically placed both his hands on my shoulders, inspecting me for wounds. "Dave, I hope you're all right," he said, "That must have been quite a shock. You look like you survived."

"Oh, I'm fine," I said, "Not a scratch on me. I'll live to tell the tale."

Indeed, I am writing it now.

10

Thanks be to God, Jon had no recollection of his encounter with Mourning. I've learned children have malleable memories, which often makes it possible for them to move easily between reality and make-believe worlds. Jon woke up thinking that he'd had a vivid dream about flying, and his imagination embellished what he recalled with details that did not even actually happen. Jon remembered hurtling skyward in a rocket ship but not the demon's frightening impersonation of his dead sister's voice. The Lord protected Jon's emotions through a little boy's adventurous fantasy.

After the tornado, the shed was removed from memory, also. The day after its destruction, Joe threw it piece by piece into the back of a borrowed pickup truck, with Margaret helping him. Of course, I supervised. I wasn't exactly sure what the earthly remains of Mourning would be, so I made it a point to be on the scene, just in case a bit of supernatural burial was required. For instance, would we uncover two red, glowing eyes? And what had become of the demon's back leg that Trixie gnawed off? When the smoke cleared, as they say on Earth, Mourning had left nothing behind other than his stench.

"Ugh!" Margaret said, throwing a chunk of siding into the truck. "Joe, why didn't you tell me this shed stank to high heaven? We should've taken it away a long time ago. It smells awful!"

"You can smell that?" I said.

Margaret grimaced. "They can smell that clear over in Jersey!" she replied, pinching her nostrils.

Well, now, Maggie could also detect evil supernaturally. Her Bible reading was transforming her spiritual nose. The wisdom of God was just blossoming all around me, in contrast to the Pennsylvania foliage that was beginning its annual crispy-orange shrivel in the late-September air. Something American mortals referred to as "the holidays" was approaching.

This season excited the Hanson family, beginning with what they called "Halloween." By listening to Jon's gleeful jabbering about it—the candy, the costumes—I got the gist of what the night was about. Why parents would glorify the realm of the occult by dressing up their children for it and feeding them celebratory sugar to acknowledge it was more than I, as a holy angel, could understand. To me, the Halloween holiday was a dangerous invitation to the Lord's enemies to come and play with the babies.

But a full three weeks before the designated night of the dead, every house in the Hansons' neighborhood was systematically and thoroughly festooned with imitation cobwebs. Humble pumpkins that were simply minding their own business in the garden patch were yanked from their vines and hollowed out and stuffed with burning candles. Black cardboard cats, their claws extended with what looked like electrified menace, were taped to windows in copious numbers, an invasion to which I thought Trixie might object, but no. Pipe-cleaner spiders, amorphous ghosts twisted from bed sheets, and fiberboard tombstones were placed throughout the yards and given inordinate amounts of attention. And don't even get me started about the zombies! Everybody seemed to believe it was all right to party with the deceased, which made me upset, and I said so. King Saul in the Old Testament came to a bad end for just such forbidden activities. He should never have consulted the Witch of Endor!

"How come Dave's so grumpy?" Joe asked Maggie one night.

"It seems he doesn't approve of *Halloween,*" she said with emphasis, taking a candied apple off a cookie sheet that dripped with a sticky glaze. "It seems he's *superstitious,*" she added.

"I am not superstitious," I replied. "I am right." The pair might have come far enough spiritually to smell demons, but they needed to get their holidays straight.

Because of my explicitly dour opinion of the evening, I got to babysit the house on Halloween. Jon did not want someone trick-or-treating with him who glared at every goblin who walked by, or who kept saying loudly, "The Lord rebuke thee!" over and over. It seems I was viewed as a killjoy. I might even use my cane to poke a mummy, they feared. Thus, I was not permitted to walk around the neighborhood with the Hansons, and, instead, I got assigned to handing out candy at the family's front door.

This duty was not a perfect occupation for me, either, since I was prone to ignoring the doorbell, just for spite. I preferred to sit in the den, playing sacred music on my trumpet to stake out my territory and to remind any evil spirits floating around that Most High is in charge, so forget it. When one obnoxious boy refused to stop pounding on the door, however, I got up from my chair testily. I came face-to-face with a short person attired in a frogman's costume representative of something called a "Navy SEAL."

I'm afraid I lost my composure at such a sight, considering what my adopted family had just been through. "No more toads!" I screamed, which frightened the child into hysterics and made him want to dress as a "rock star" the following year, which his mother did not consider an improvement, and for which I was also blamed. (I don't care.)

Then there was "Thanksgiving." These American holidays baffled me. I was just as patriotic as the next guardian-in-training, but I found that I simply could not bring myself to eat a fellow winged creature, the turkey. Thankfully, for Thanksgiving, people had the good sense to use pumpkins for their God-given purpose and put them into delicious pies fragrant with nutmeg and cinnamon. Any holiday with baked goods is fine by me! But consuming the turkey, especially when they sawed off its wings in front of me at the table, was outside my ability to compromise.

"Dave, would you like a nice, meaty wing?" Joe had asked me, presenting the appendage on a silver platter. (He had no remorse at all, it appeared.)

"I'll just have pie and a glass of warm milk," I responded. "Thanks, though. My stomach's a little unsettled." In fact, I was dizzy.

I thought we were really on to something with "Christmas." Celebrating the Lord's birthday! What a great idea! Why not? Mortals celebrated everyone else's birthday, so why not God's? I was not aware at the time that Jesus had a birthday, but this ignorance I attributed to my young age and inexperience. I was overjoyed that human beings had shown a modicum of wisdom by recognizing the Lord, and if they wanted to do so in a birthday tradition, so much the better.

Now up until this time in my life, I had been studying the Old Testament, only. I knew Christ because he created me in heaven, and through the teachings of Isaiah the prophet, in which Father God had instructed me. Frankly, many of those lessons were mysterious to me, and difficult to comprehend, but I entrusted both my knowledge and my ignorance to the goodness of God. Imagine the exultant state of my emotions when I learned that God's Word includes another whole book, the New Testament, and that it emphasizes Jesus! At this discovery, I felt nothing other than jubilation that there was actually more of the Bible to love.

Here is how I learned of the New Covenant: I found Margaret reading the Christmas story in the book of Luke one morning, early, while drinking her coffee. She was shy about being seen with the New Testament, as many new believers are. In their self-consciousness, they're aware that something about them is different than it used to be and that the difference is apparent to those who are close to them.

"What have you got there? The next best-seller?" I said, pulling up a chair beside my friend. I looked around for the cream and sugar.

"I was going to read a chapter privately."

The hint was lost on me. I was hungry. "In what? May I use the toaster?"

"It's the New Testament. The book of Luke. You know, the story of Jesus's birth."

I dropped my coffee cup. "The what? That's in there? Let me see!"

"Dave, you're acting like you've never seen a New Testament before!"

I did everything but take the book right out of Maggie's hands to gobble it up, forget the toast. But she was so visibly disappointed at losing her devotional time with the Bible, I reluctantly gave her back her book. She teased me about it. "You can always go to the library, Dave," she said. "I think you know where it is."

While I waited for my chance to read the New Testament, I was pleased to participate with Joe Hanson in activities that were Christmas-related. For instance, there was the odd custom of bringing a tree indoors and trimming it with jewel-toned balls, miniature toys, and yards and yards of silken, braided ropes. During the frosty expedition to fell a tree, Joe talked about his Norwegian relatives' Christmas parties, and so I came to understand that the holiday is celebrated all over the world, and that, indeed, in some countries, the trees are decorated with real, burning candles. Upon hearing that bit of information, my guardian's nature was immediately aroused. Surely the story was folklore, given the combustible equation of pine needles plus flames multiplied by hot, sputtering wax.

But, when in Rome... I discreetly created a fire extinguisher and disciplined my form, Dave, into showing nothing but appreciation for illogically bringing trees of the forest inside and setting them on fire with candles, which Joe was compelled to demonstrate for my cultural education. I also withheld my disdain for the dainty, sparkling female angel perched on top of the Hansons' tree in her waft of tulle and crinoline. And the being "Santa Claus" was beyond the pale. I saw him on television. What a poseur!

Like any birthday party, Christmas included presents galore. For the children everywhere in the world, this was the best part—alas, for the Hansons, that year gift giving was the tender spot of their grief. Only one child would receive presents the Christmas I stayed with my family. Without Hannah, the season was marred with sadness. For Jonathan's sake, Joe and Margaret resolutely took part in the holiday, though it was muted in its observance. Despite their heartache, the parents hung Hannah's stocking on the fireplace mantel. Jon could not look at the sock without bursting into tears.

I noticed that the imagery of a baby boy was prominent in the Hansons' Christmas decorations, many still stored willy-nilly in a cumbersome, plastic tub until they were displayed. I believed the baby to be a portrayal of Jesus as an infant, since it was his birthday. But when Joe, Maggie, and Jon gathered on Christmas Eve to present me with a holiday gift, I had to excuse myself to sit in stunned silence, alone. The growing pains of spiritual maturity were about to afflict me again.

At Jon's insistence, because of the encroaching cold weather, I had moved indoors from the screen porch and had made a small, cozy corner of the den my own. I sat down wearily in my rocking chair and wept like an orphan while opening my present. I was absolutely stupefied. My family stood before me at a respectful distance, terribly concerned.

For there on the Christmas card that came with the fresh, white tube socks Jon presented so lovingly was etched in gold ink an earth-shattering poem. I read it ruefully. The Hanson family never noticed the verses, but the poem changed my universe. I sat in my corner, rocking, shivering, and barely able to speak with the Holy Spirit.

You have been keeping this from me, I prayed, crestfallen. *Are there no birthdays on this planet that aren't horrific?* Over my lap, I spread open the Christmas card for the Spirit to read:

'Lowly Jesus, raised in Nazareth,
Born to die, as ransom paid for human death.
Nailed to a tree, so that man might live,
On your birthday, Lord, all praise we give...'

Why didn't you tell me? was all I could pray. *My Lord Christ is killed?*

This is why you could not know before, the Spirit murmured. *Without your help, another little boy will die.*

For at that moment, Jonathan came to me in his Superman pajamas and climbed up on my knees. He took my face in his little hands. "Don't you like your present, Uncle Dave?" he asked.

"No, it's not that," I replied. I hugged the boy tightly. "Jon, I just found out that someone I love more than anybody died."

Jon reached up, and with his young, supple fingers, he gently wiped the tears from my eyes. "I know how you feel," he said. "I loved Hannah, and she went away, too."

I nodded. There is kinship in grief.

Margaret and Joe waited not knowing what to do, watchful of this interaction, and empathetic. They trusted me with Jon. Whatever was bothering me, they knew I would profit from some of their son's innocent affection.

An hour passed. I rocked Jon. I prayed.

Unable to remain so still anymore, at length the boy crawled off my lap and walked to the plastic tub containing the family's collection of decorations for all the annual holidays. What a jumble! Every American household has such a tub. It was overflowing, a riot of patterned tablecloths and matching place mats, knots of electric lights, paper hats, Scotch tape, scissors, and special-occasion stationery. To Jon, the tub was a toy box, and he began to pull out objects from it and stack them in heaps on the floor. "You'll feel better if we play," he said to me.

My eye caught a delicate greeting card with a shimmering cross on the front. Mortals seem to make much of sentimental cards, and this one was so beautiful that I pulled it from the pile of decorations to see it better. Upon closer inspection, I saw that the cross was outlined in red silk, and it was superimposed over a hillside. The card was blank. Inside, it contained no message. It was obviously intended for writing a personal note. On the front of the card, however, above the cross, were the emblazoned words, "He is Risen. Have a Blessed Easter."

My pulse quickened.

"Jon," I implored, motioning for him to come to stand in front of me. "Would you tell me about Easter? Tell me everything you know."

"You're funny," the child giggled. "You know more than me. You're old!"

"Make believe that I'm a friend from a faraway land, and I never saw Easter even one time. What would you say?"

"There's candy and bunnies and baskets…"

"Is that all? Isn't there something else?" I said, holding the Easter card in my hand. I searched the boy's face. "Try to remember, Jon. I need to know."

The boy stared at the ceiling, fidgeting. Then, the sun rose again in my world.

"Baby Jesus comes back to life!" Jon cried out. "Timmy at kindergarten told me!"

"I knew it! I just knew it!" I shouted, lifting the boy high into the air. "It couldn't be the end! God would never permit it!"

"Looks like Dave's himself again," Joe said, taking a long drink of eggnog.

I swung Jon around the room, exulting in my new knowledge of the ultimate goal of Christmas. "Yay, Easter!" Jon yelled.

"All right, all right," Margaret interrupted jovially. "It's still Christmas everybody. No more swinging if you don't want to get on the naughty list."

It was just as well. I felt a sudden, excruciating jolt, a shooting pain in my chest. *Holy Spirit, what is this I'm feeling?* I prayed anxiously. I had never experienced pain in that place in my body before.

Gabriel, your form is only flesh, came the reply.

Slowly, I went back to my rocker and took a deep breath. I said nothing. I didn't want to ruin Christmas for the Hansons. It was already a difficult time, without Hannah. The ache in my chest subsided. I settled down.

But I understood that with the New Year, change would come.

11

By firelight, I was barely sustained through the winter. I recoiled at the cold weather, which seemed brutal to me, and as the gray, frosty days blended one into another, my form, Dave, grew sleepy, then weak. Sitting in my rocking chair, often with my trumpet lying near me, I endured the snow that thrashed against the house as if it wanted to take my place near the hearth. February is the bleakest month in Clayton, Pennsylvania. In heaven, we have no seasons of decline.

The Holy Spirit came to visit me frequently. He himself travels as a flame, and sometimes I could not tell who was warming me, the Spirit or the logs. I needed warming. It was winter in Dave's bones. His impermanent, mortal senses were fading away like the dying hardwood embers in the fireplace. If Dave had been a real man, and not a verisimilar form that I created for a godly purpose, he would have realized that a full life was behind him. As he was, I could tell that the flesh I'd assumed for my mission was winding down, as was my assignment on Earth.

One snowy morning as I sat on my deep chair cushions and rocked, Jonathan came running to me for a music lesson. This day, he didn't want to learn to read the notes. He had no patience for details like that. He just wanted to blast out short bursts from the trumpet. I smiled to myself. Jon was exploring his strength, a definite step toward eventual manhood, and I was relieved that his well-being could now be gauged by the decibels of trumpet bursts and not the depth or number of holes he dug in the dirt with a spoon. Jon had passed through his own deadly winter, which he'd encountered so early in his life, and come out on the other side of it, still alive, still young, ready to make the most of his time in the spring.

When we were done with playing, I snapped shut my trumpet case with its extravagant red silk lining and handed the instrument to the boy. "This is yours now," I said decisively. "I want you to practice on it every day. Will you do that for me, Jon?"

The boy's eyes widened. "I can't take this, Uncle Dave," he said. "It's your special jazz horn. How come you don't want it anymore?"

I looked at Jon through eyes of love. "I've been thinking about moving on from jazz. Growing in different ways is important. But you're a jazz man if I ever saw one. You keep that horn, Jon."

The boy stared at me, then looked at the case, then carried the trumpet to his bedroom. The instrument filled both his arms to capacity as he struggled to wrap them around it. That's the way it should be with a passion, any God-given passion. It should so fill up one's heart as to be almost overwhelming, almost too big to carry inside one, and require a lifetime of positive, healthy effort to lift it up and master it. Otherwise, a passion becomes only a burden, especially if one is alone.

When I began to believe that March's winter had become eternal, it melted off in a single day. April came. It arrived with icicles snapping in half in the sunshine and the small, lithe creatures peeking out of their holes. Young were birthed. Soon the grass once more turned green, and, in May, the foliage sprouted exuberantly with buds and flowers. Margaret opened up the screen porch again, and Joe talked of power washing the house. Jonathan searched for his sandals, anticipating time at the beach in June.

The Holy Spirit came to me one night with a whisper. I was asleep in my chair, but I knew his voice. *It's time to lay down your cane, Gabriel.* The month was July. I had seen all that the world's seasons had to offer in one year. I had learned what it is to be a human being and had observed the brokenness in man that had motivated my Lord Jesus to give himself on a cross. Though to the mortal eye I was aging and my body was past its prime, in God's eyes, I was only beginning my best work. It was time to move on.

The Spirit was right to call me, of course. I awoke and turned on a small lamp. There in the half-light, I saw the few clothes I kept neatly folded in a basket in my corner. I saw my cane hanging on the back of the rocking chair where I often slept on plush cushions. My trumpet was fondly bequeathed to Jon to bring him comfort at my departure. There was little material wealth for me to leave behind. I had not encumbered myself with possessions, but I was no longer a homeless garbage man in any way. I had been taken in and loved.

Knowing that everyone in the Hanson home was sound asleep, and that they wouldn't see, I shed the form Dave and rocked in my chair unfettered, remembering, reminiscing, with my angelic aura filling the den with golden light. I said a silent farewell to my family. In the morning, they would find Dave at peace. *Lord, bless and protect the Hansons,* I prayed. *Please give Joe and Maggie the right words for Jon.*

I left as I came, through the screen porch.

I departed just as my replacement spread his sheltering, celestial wings over the Hansons' roof, for Jesus would not leave the heirs of salvation unguarded.

Then, in a twinkling, I was home in heaven. Time had moved forward, into the future. Years had passed on planet Earth.

The Lord Jesus met me by the Lake of Insight. He was carrying Trixie!

I knelt at the feet of Christ. I knew so much more about him, now. I understood so much more of his great sacrifice, the most important sacrifice ever made. But I had one unanswered question about my assignment. "Why did I train with Jonathan, Lord?" I asked. I thought perhaps the boy might have become a great pastor or a brave missionary. I wondered if his parents were somehow distinctive in God's eyes.

"Because he's Jonathan," Jesus said, "Because he's important to me, and I love him."

Jon didn't need to be special. He was Jon, and that was enough for God.

Wriggling now from being held, Trixie began to bark. The little creature insisted that Most High pay attention.

"No, I haven't forgotten, Trixie," the Lord laughed. He placed the renewed, completely healed dog into the ethereal grass. No more limp for Trixie! The Lord smiled and clapped his hands. "Standish! Come here, boy!" he called. And out of the forest ran the most beautiful male, copper-colored dachshund imaginable—and he was followed by a litter of six tumbling puppies.

"What Trixie was never able to have on Earth, you provided in heaven." I reached over to pat the dog's head and rub her ears.

"And speaking of time on Earth," the Lord responded. "Gabriel, you did well. I promote you today to herald status. You're going to need this," Jesus said, handing me a brand-new trumpet. "I made one for you in solid gold, but with no carrying case this time. No need for you to ever put it away again. Make good use of it."

"Thank you, Lord," I said. "I will play it always in your honor."

Lord Jesus held me close for a moment. Then he looked down at Earth. "Gabriel, don't you have places to be?"

"Yes, Lord," I replied. "I have read the New Testament."

"Go, then. Fulfill your calling. You're ready."

Back, back, back, I flew, thousands of years to the temple in Jerusalem to speak to the old priest, Zechariah. He and his wife, Elizabeth, were to be especially blessed. I knew just what to say, for I was familiar with the ways of the aged. Zechariah was speechless at the news that elderly Elizabeth would bear a son called John, the Baptizer, but it all worked out at their home in Hebron.

Next, on to Nazareth I went, in Galilee, into the home of a virgin named Mary. I knew just how to gain her attention, for I had once been a teenage girl, myself: "Greetings, you who are highly favored. You will conceive and bear a son named Jesus."

Then, still in Nazareth, I flew into the dreams of a man named Joseph, who was unsure about his upcoming marriage to Mary. I knew just what to say, for I had experience giving spiritual advice to troubled, middle-aged men who were worried about their livelihood and reputation.

I prayed for all these, with respect and compassion, for I knew what lay ahead for them as they lost their beloved child. I had learned the lesson of mourning in Clayton, Pennsylvania.

And, finally, on to Judea I winged, to Bethlehem, to prepare for Jesus's debut in a shed full of animals, wise men, and shepherds. I knew just what to say at that event, for I knew about being outdoors with nowhere to go, dependent on strangers for love.

Such was my greatest appointment.

After that, I took up my trumpet and made my way back to heaven.

There. I have put down the scribe's writing reed. The story of my spiritual training is complete. I will send a copy to the Hansons for their review.

I must pause to reflect on beginning another book.

I have time. I will always have time.

Should I tell about my visits to Daniel?

Or perhaps I will write a novel...

If you enjoyed reading this book, please consider writing a positive review of it online at Goodreads, Amazon, or Barnes & Noble.com. Thank you!

ABOUT THE AUTHOR

Diane Rosier Miles lives on the invisible border between the everyday world and the spacious vista of her imagination. This territory has been a surprise to Diane and sometimes a confusing place, but since it's the country where she feels most at home, she decided long ago to claim citizenship, roll with its challenges, and write.

Diane crafts tales for readers who are drawn to the supernatural presence of God in the imponderable joys, doubts, and sorrows of human existence, particularly of family life. Diane's stories often include traditional spiritual themes and an appreciation of the mystical.

In addition to writing, Diane bakes cakes and is not at all discouraged in that activity by being left-handed. To share a recipe or just a good word, contact Diane at dianerosiermiles@gmail.com.

71529022R00066

Made in the USA
Middletown, DE
25 April 2018